STARK LIBRARY

JUN -- 2023

DISCARD

TEEN CHALLENGES

BULLYING

by Carol Hand

CONTENT CONSULTANT
Dr. Samantha Coyle
Assistant Professor, Psychology
Montclair State University

An Imprint of Abdo Publishing | abdobooks.com

ABDOBOOKS.COM

Published by Abdo Publishing, a division of ABDO, PO Box 398166, Minneapolis, Minnesota 55439. Copyright © 2022 by Abdo Consulting Group, Inc. International copyrights reserved in all countries. No part of this book may be reproduced in any form without written permission from the publisher. Essential Library™ is a trademark and logo of Abdo Publishing.

Printed in the United States of America, North Mankato, Minnesota.
102021
012022

THIS BOOK CONTAINS RECYCLED MATERIALS

Cover Photo: Shutterstock Images
Interior Photos: Shutterstock Images, 4, 12, 18, 27; Monkey Business Images/iStockphoto, 8; Georgia Court/iStockphoto, 16; Monkey Business Images/Shutterstock Images, 22–23, 66; Syda Productions/Shutterstock Images, 24; Chainarong Prasertthai/iStockphoto, 32; LightField Studios/Shutterstock Images, 34; iStockphoto, 38–39, 53, 55, 88, 96; Marcos Calvo/iStockphoto, 41; Courtney Hale/iStockphoto, 46; FatCamera/iStockphoto, 50; 002 Images/Alamy, 56; Kirk Treakle/Alamy, 60–61; DGLimages/iStockphoto, 65; PR Pictures Production/Shutterstock Images, 70; Prostock-Studio/iStockphoto, 74, 76–77; Motortion Films/Shutterstock Images, 78; SDI Productions/iStockphoto, 80, 84; SolStock/iStockphoto, 90; Roger Harris/Science Source, 94; Richard Milnes/Alamy, 99

Editor: Alyssa Krekelberg
Series Designer: Colleen McLaren

LIBRARY OF CONGRESS CONTROL NUMBER: 2021941244

PUBLISHER'S CATALOGING-IN-PUBLICATION DATA

Names: Hand, Carol, author.

Title: Bullying / by Carol Hand

Description: Minneapolis, Minnesota : Abdo Publishing, 2022 | Series: Teen challenges | Includes online resources and index.

Identifiers: ISBN 9781532196263 (lib. bdg.) | ISBN 9781098218072 (ebook)

Subjects: LCSH: Bullying--Juvenile literature. | Bullying in schools--Juvenile literature. | Students--Conduct of life--Juvenile literature. | Problem solving--Juvenile literature. | School violence--Prevention--Juvenile literature.

Classification: DDC 302.34--dc23

CONTENTS

CHAPTER ONE
BEING BULLIED 04

CHAPTER TWO
WHAT IS BULLYING? 12

CHAPTER THREE
EFFECTS OF BULLYING . . . 24

Trigger warning: This chapter presents information about suicide.

CHAPTER FOUR
WHO GETS BULLIED? 34

CHAPTER FIVE
WHY DOES
BULLYING HAPPEN? 46

CHAPTER SIX
A HISTORY OF BULLYING . . . 56

CHAPTER SEVEN
THE BULLY AND
THE BYSTANDER 66

CHAPTER EIGHT
OVERCOMING BULLYING . . . 78

CHAPTER NINE
PROMISING RESEARCH 90

ESSENTIAL FACTS 100
GLOSSARY 102
ADDITIONAL RESOURCES 104
SOURCE NOTES 106
INDEX 110
ABOUT THE AUTHOR 112
ABOUT THE CONSULTANT 112

Getting bullied can be deeply upsetting, and it can happen to anyone.

CHAPTER ONE

BEING BULLIED

Alexa rushed into the bathroom. She was trying to hold back her tears until she was safely hidden in a stall. This year, it seemed like several girls in Alexa's grade had made it their mission to constantly gang up on her. She knew she wasn't in their popular social group, but why couldn't they just leave her alone? Alexa wasn't bothering them. In fact, she tried her best to stay out of their way. But she couldn't avoid them in the hallways or in the cafeteria. After getting picked on every day at lunch for what felt like forever, Alexa decided to skip going to the cafeteria and spend the lunch period in the bathroom instead. But when lunch was over, she always had to face them again when they passed in the hallway.

    Sitting alone in the quiet bathroom, Alexa kept asking herself how this situation even started. The leaders of the group, Marisa and Jennifer, had been her friends last year in eighth grade. They had sleepovers, watched movies, practiced doing makeup, and giggled over boys they thought were cute. But over the summer they didn't hang out as much. Marisa and Jennifer both took long vacations with their families, and once they were back in

PEOPLE WHO ARE BULLIED

Anyone can be the victim of bullying. Bullies often turn their cruelty on people who are different or who stand out in any way. Young teens can be very sensitive about their physical appearance, so any prominent trait—such as weight, body shape, or disability—may be something that a bully targets. People can also be victimized for other reasons, such as for being shy. Members of minority racial groups or religions, or those with different sexual orientations from those of the bullies, are often targeted as well. No one deserves to be bullied. Differences between people are important and can make a community more enriched. Instead of being made to feel ashamed for their differences, people should learn to love themselves for who they are.

town, Alexa was busy in marching band camp.

On the first day of high school, Marisa and Jennifer attached themselves to a new group of friends. They were all thin and wore stylish clothes. Alexa had no new clothes and had gained just a little weight over the summer. Marisa and Jennifer's new group also had a new favorite activity: making fun of Alexa. The girls called her fatty, piggy, and loser. They sent her Instagram pictures of actual pigs. They laughed and whispered about her in the hallways. Alexa was confused and upset. Not only had she lost her friends but they had also turned against her for no reason.

OPENING UP

That day, Alexa was nearly late to English class, and her teacher noticed her red face and puffy eyes. Ms. Hart kept her after class to ask whether everything was OK. The concern in Ms. Hart's eyes led Alexa to tell her everything.

The bullying didn't stop, but Alexa felt better talking to someone about what she was going through. Ms. Hart was not only sympathetic but also insisted there were ways to improve the situation. She took Alexa to see the school counselor, and they set up meetings where Alexa could talk about what was happening. They discussed ways to assert herself and even respond to her bullies. Mostly, Alexa learned to feel better about herself. Developing self-confidence was hard, but she began to understand that she did not deserve to be bullied.

The counselor also called Alexa's parents and brought them to school to discuss the situation. Her parents were upset that she had not told them, and Alexa explained how embarrassed she had felt. They assured her that the bullying was not her fault, and they encouraged her to talk to them about it. The principal talked to Marisa, Jennifer, and the other girls and told them

> "A BIG, HUGE PART OF THIS BULLYING PROBLEM IS SOCIAL MEDIA. THESE KIDS ARE HIDING BEHIND A COMPUTER SCREEN."[1]
> —WENDY DEL MONTE, PARENT OF A BULLIED TEEN

If someone is being bullied, she should speak to a trusted adult, such as a school guidance counselor, teacher, or parent.

disciplinary action would be taken if the bullying didn't stop. Soon after, the bullying episodes died down. They didn't go away entirely, but Alexa was getting better at walking past the bullies with her head held high, saying nothing.

    Alexa also established new friendships. She saw Ellie reading alone at lunch one day, so she sat down and introduced herself. After that, the two of them began to hang out, and the fact that Alexa had a new friend seemed to discourage the bullies from picking on her. She was glad she had talked to Ms. Hart. And she was glad she hadn't let the bullies win and ruin her year.

A COMPLEX PROBLEM

Bullying is different from joking or teasing. Bullying tends to involve an imbalance of power, which means the bully is, or appears to be, more powerful than the victim. The bully might be larger and stronger, have a higher social status, or just be more aggressive. Or a group of kids might gang up on a single victim.

Bullying is not a onetime thing. Whether they are calling people names, spreading rumors, or tripping victims in the hallway, bullies do the same actions over and over. In addition, bullying is not accidental. The bully deliberately targets the victim and intends to cause harm. Bullying is not a joke. It hurts people, and the cruelty can haunt victims for years afterward.

Bullying is complex. In order to understand this problem, people need to understand what

> "BULLYING USUALLY ISN'T A ONETIME ACT. RATHER, IT REPRESENTS AN ONGOING PATTERN OF BEHAVIOR."[2]
> —SHERRI GORDON, WRITER AND BULLYING PREVENTION EXPERT

WHAT ARE BULLIES LIKE?

A paper from the journal *School Psychology Review* noted that about 30 percent of young people admit that they have bullied others.[3] Bullies lash out at those who are fearful, submissive, and unable to assert themselves. Bullies may misread or fail to understand others' feelings or attitudes. They often have problems with parents as well as peers. But bullies do not fall neatly into a single category. They have different personalities, and their bullying has different goals, motivations, and behaviors.

Dr. Mary C. Lamia, a clinical psychologist, also explains the role that shame plays in a bully's actions: "Psychologists have found that kids who behave like bullies . . . are very 'shame-prone.' That means they are afraid their failures or shortcomings will be exposed. . . . Their mean behavior toward others keeps their self-esteem high because it takes . . . others' attention away from the parts of themselves about which they are ashamed."[4]

it is and how it can be identified. They can also look into the history of bullying and see how long this issue has been around. In addition, it's important to understand how bullying affects both the victim and the perpetrator at the time of the incidents and later in life. People who are being bullied and bystanders who see it occurring should also know what can be done about bullying. Can it be stopped or controlled? If so, what methods work best?

Bullying is a serious problem in schools as well as in neighborhoods or on the playground. Most times, it happens when adults are not present. It is also increasingly happening online through texting and social networking apps commonly used by teens. This type of bullying can be very harmful and is known as cyberbullying.

Bullying is not simple or easy to deal with, and it can have long-term consequences for both the victim and the bully. But understanding how and why bullying happens can be the first step toward controlling it. Learning how to effectively handle bullying can make a teen's life more comfortable for learning and for growing up.

THE RISE OF CYBERBULLYING

In a study by the National Center for Education Statistics, 20 percent of middle and high school students polled said they were bullied during the 2016 school year. Of these students, 15 percent said they were bullied through texts or online.[5] Between 2014 and 2016, cyberbullying increased from 11.5 to 15.3 percent. Three times as many girls as boys were cyberbullied. This included 21 percent of middle and high school girls who said they were bullied compared to less than 7 percent of boys.[6]

Bullies sometimes use text messages or social media to harass their victims.

CHAPTER TWO

WHAT IS BULLYING?

Sometimes people aren't sure whether they are being bullied or teased, and there can be a fine line between the two. Everyone, including the victim, bully, and bystanders, should be aware that if an interaction is meant to hurt another person or is repeated over and over, it is bullying. It is not innocent, harmless, or done by accident. Also, a bully always has power over the victim.

Teasing or joking is typically done with a good-natured intent and is not meant to harm the person being teased. It involves making fun of someone in a playful way and is usually a onetime thing. However, Sherri Gordon, a bullying prevention expert, notes that sometimes there isn't much difference between teasing and bullying: "Sometimes playfully teasing someone or making fun of them is not so fun after all, especially if the person on the receiving end does not find it funny. When this happens, this is . . . a subtle form of bullying."[1]

Hazing is another thing people might experience at school. It involves many of the same types of behaviors as bullying and should not be tolerated. During hazing, a person might be required to do a humiliating or even dangerous act as part of an initiation into a group, such as a sorority, fraternity, or club. The University of Michigan notes, "Hazing is often about power and control. . . . Individuals cannot consent to being hazed because hazing is illegal [in most states]."[2]

TYPES OF BULLYING

Statistics on the frequency of bullying vary slightly, depending on the source of the information. But in a 2017 report, the National Center for Education Statistics and the Bureau of Justice Statistics stated that about 20 percent of US students have been bullied. So, approximately one in five students will experience bullying.[3]

Bullying occurs in many ways. Physical bullying is when the bully kicks, punches, shoves, or otherwise physically assaults a victim. Verbal bullying involves the use of words to insult, demean, or otherwise hurt someone. Emotional bullying, also called relational aggression,

MEANNESS VS. BULLYING

It is sometimes difficult to tell the difference between bullying and simple meanness because they involve similar types of behavior. Bullying involves a difference in power or social standing, while meanness occurs between two people of equal social standing. If a girl insults her best friend, this is meanness. But if she picks on a younger girl who doesn't fit in because of the clothes she wears, for example, she is bullying the younger girl.

is different from verbal bullying. It involves actions such as spreading rumors, ostracizing a victim from a group, or breaking confidences. Cyberbullying is the use of technology to hurt or harass victims. It may involve posting images, texts, or threats on social media. Sexual bullying includes crude comments or gestures, unwanted touching, or shaming someone for perceived promiscuity. Prejudicial bullying is directed at another person due to factors such as his or her race, religion, or sexual orientation.

> "CHILDREN, FOR ALL THEIR INNOCENCE AND INEXPERIENCE OF THE WORLD, CAN BE SOME OF THE MOST VICIOUS BULLIES. THEIR ACTIONS, PERHAPS LESS HINDERED BY THE SOCIAL NORMS WE LEARN IN LATER LIFE, CAN BE MERCILESS, VIOLENT AND SHOCKING. AND THEY CAN HAVE LIFE-LONG IMPLICATIONS FOR THE VICTIMS."[4]
>
> —KELLY OAKES, WRITER FOR THE BBC

It is important to understand and recognize all types of bullying. That way, people—including teachers, parents, friends, bystanders, or the victim—can take steps to help stop the bullying. If people don't report bullying, it often goes unrecognized, and the victim continues to suffer.

Physical bullying is the easiest form to recognize. Others can see a bully punch, kick, or shove someone.

A bullying victim may be excluded from group activities.

Even if the assault is not seen, its effects may be visible. Physical bullies are often bigger, stronger, and more aggressive than their victims. Because physical bullying is so outwardly apparent, it is the most studied. It's also the type of bullying to which schools most often respond.

Other types of bullying, such as verbal and relational aggression, are more difficult to notice. Therefore, adults are more likely to miss the signs of these forms of bullying. Verbal abuse often involves name-calling to belittle the victim. It can also involve taunting, inappropriate comments, or even threats. In relational aggression, bullies want to improve their own social standing by bringing down others. They do this by manipulating situations in order to exclude a person from a group or by forcing someone out of a group. They may embarrass the victims in public or tell others not to be friends with them. Verbal and relational bullying can be easily missed. That's because if an adult or bystander doesn't hear what's being said, it might not look like anything is wrong. In addition, if confronted, a bully can lie and claim that he or she was only teasing.

GENDER AND RELATIONAL AGGRESSION

Researchers have found mixed results when studying which gender uses relational aggression more. Some say that girls are more relationally aggressive, while others note that boys are. Different studies say that there's no gender differences relating to this form of bullying at all, and that both genders use it equally. However, a study published in *Behavioral Sciences* notes, "Relational aggression, on its own, may be particularly important to look at in girls, because these aggressive tactics appear to negatively affect girls more than they affect boys."[5] The study goes on to note that girls who engage in relational aggression have less empathy and might have adjustment issues.

CYBERBULLYING

Cyberbullying utilizes cell phones, tablets, and computers. It can occur through a wide variety of online media, including text messages, instant messages, online apps,

Bullying in the digital age is not confined to schools. Many teens experience cyberbullying, which can reach them at any time of the day.

and emails. It can occur through social media such as Facebook, Twitter, Snapchat, and Instagram, or in forums or online games. It can involve written messages, photos, videos, or personal information sent to harm, harass, embarrass, or threaten someone.

Cyberbullying takes abuse to a whole new level. First of all, traditional bullying is often restricted to a certain area, such as in school. But cyberbullying can happen at all times of the day and week. The bully can be anonymous while online, so the victim isn't always sure who is targeting him.

Also, if a bully posts hurtful messages about her victim in a public forum, the victim can't be sure how many people have read the negative information. Many social media sites have policies that aim to keep their users safe. If a bully is in violation of these policies, the victim can report the individual. The person being bullied can also block the user.

Some types of online abuse are illegal in many states, and the perpetrator can face serious legal trouble if caught. This is especially true if the abuse involves discrimination against a person because of that person's race, religion, gender,

CYBERBULLYING CONCERNS

The US government website Stop Bullying notes that cyberbullying has additional effects on both the bully and the victim that other forms of bullying don't have. The site states:

The content an individual shares online—both their personal content as well as any negative, mean, or hurtful content—creates a kind of permanent public record of their views, activities, and behavior. This public record can be thought of as an online reputation, which may be accessible to schools, employers, colleges, clubs, and others who may be researching an individual now or in the future. Cyberbullying can harm the online reputations of everyone involved—not just the person being bullied, but those doing the bullying or participating in it.[6]

sexual orientation, or physical differences. Ruth Carter, an attorney, says, "Depending on the rules of your state and the circumstances involved, discipline can include expulsion from school, criminal charges for harassment and/or civil lawsuits for defamation and other harms."[7]

SEXTING

Sexting is digitally sending or receiving sexually explicit material, including messages, photos, or videos, primarily by cell phone. Sexting may seem harmless. But once sent, a message can't be retrieved. And sexually explicit messages might be distributed to people other than the original recipient. For example, if a couple had a bad breakup, one person might share a very personal image of the other with friends in order to harm his or her ex. If a sexual photo shows someone younger than 18 years old, it is considered child pornography. Sending or sharing images like this is a crime.

SEXUAL AND PREJUDICIAL BULLYING

Bullying often happens when the bully wants to hurt or demean a person because he or she is different in some way from the bully. Two common types of bullying that result from this attitude are sexual bullying and prejudicial bullying. Targets of sexual bullying are usually women. But this form of sexual harassment also significantly affects lesbian, gay, bisexual, transgender, and queer or questioning (LGBTQ) individuals.

Targets are often harassed by men who call them sexually inappropriate names, proposition them, or touch them without permission. But women may target other women, calling them demeaning names such as slut or insulting their bodies or appearance.

According to Gordon, sexual bullying by either individuals or groups, especially when adults are not around, is a growing concern. Sexual bullying can include sexual jokes, comments, or gestures; sexually explicit name-calling; touching or grabbing the victim's body or clothing; spreading sexual rumors or gossip; posting sexually explicit comments, photos, or videos on social media; or publicly shaming the victim. Sexual bullying may make the bullies feel more powerful, or they might think their actions will raise their social status. Also, if they have been sexually bullied themselves, bullying a younger, weaker person may build up their own self-confidence. Boys might bully girls to try to convince their peers of their own sexual maturity. Girls might bully other girls out of jealousy.

> "WHEN CHILDREN ARE LOOKING FOR SOMEONE TO ABUSE, THEY'RE LOOKING FOR A NOTICEABLE DIFFERENCE. THAT PERSON MAY BE AN UNUSUALLY HIGH ACHIEVER OR COULD BE SOMEONE BELONGING TO A SENSITIVE GROUP."[8]
> —ELIZABETH ENGLANDER, PROFESSOR, BRIDGEWATER STATE COLLEGE

Despite the reasons behind it, sexual bullying is never acceptable.

Another type of bullying targets people because of who they are or what group they belong to. This is called prejudicial bullying. It stems from the bully's prejudice against someone who is different from him or her. Individuals who are bullied may belong to a different race, ethnicity, or religion, or they may be members of the LGBTQ community. Prejudicial bullying is often based on stereotypes, which are oversimplified and incorrect ideas about a specific group.

Bullying is widespread and can affect almost anyone. Often it is overlooked. Teens can be alert to signs of bullying and step in before it escalates. Bystanders can be kind to the person being bullied, and they can make sure adults know what is happening. If speaking up is a safe option, those who are being bullied can try to directly tell the bully to stop his or her behavior. They can also contact a trusted adult for help.

Teachers can help stop hurtful behavior by being direct with a bully and saying his actions are not acceptable.

Students might have trouble paying attention at school if they are bullied. This can affect their academic performance.

CHAPTER THREE

EFFECTS OF BULLYING

Bullying has a negative effect on the entire school community. This can result in a culture of fear, pressure, and anxiety among victims, bullies, bystanders, families, and friends. The effect on the bullied person is especially profound. The individual's physical and emotional health can be affected, and his or her academic performance and social life may suffer. He or she might have lower self-confidence and a poor self-image, and he or she may feel embarrassed and ashamed of being bullied. In the end, people who are bullied can withdraw socially, have few friends, and spend most of their time alone. However, if people are able to address the bullying, these negative effects may be alleviated or even prevented.

SIGNS OF BULLYING

Teens who are being bullied show a variety of signs or symptoms. They often do not want to attend school or ride the bus, which is where most instances of bullying occur. While at school, they may be afraid to use the bathroom or be alone in the hallway. Their grades may begin to suffer. They can become socially withdrawn, might have low self-esteem and few friends, and avoid conflict. They may be suspicious or wary of others. They may feel unlikable, unattractive, and generally inadequate. Those who experience cyberbullying might have similar symptoms.

In 2017, the *World Journal of Psychiatry* published an analysis of studies related to bullying. It noted that any type of bullying can create mental health problems such as substance abuse for the victim. Other issues that can arise include anxiety, depression, and poor mental and physical health in general.

People who are bullied can sometimes suffer physical, emotional, social, and academic damage. Bullying victims can develop eating and sleeping disorders. They may lose interest in activities they once enjoyed, and they may start to get lower grades and standardized test scores. They may

BULLYING BY THE NUMBERS

Statistics on bullying can shine a light on how frequent and serious bullying is in the United States. For example, on average, a child in the United States is bullied every seven minutes. Nine out of every ten LGBTQ students have been bullied at school. And around 5.4 million students skip school each year due to bullying.[1]

Many studies have confirmed that there is a connection between physical issues, such as stomachaches, and bullying.

participate less in school activities, and they might even skip or drop out of school.

Bullying victims can suffer physical symptoms too. The anxiety that bullying generates takes a toll on the body, resulting in more frequent symptoms of illness, including stomachaches, headaches, and ulcers. Bullying may also aggravate preexisting health conditions, such as eczema, stomach conditions, and heart conditions.

Victims may also develop a psychological condition known as learned helplessness. When this happens, they begin to feel powerless to change the situation and give up trying. This leads to severe depression and a feeling that there is no way out of their situation. However, people

> "BULLYING IS AN ATTEMPT TO INSTILL FEAR AND SELF-LOATHING. BEING THE REPETITIVE TARGET OF BULLYING DAMAGES YOUR ABILITY TO VIEW YOURSELF AS A DESIRABLE, CAPABLE AND EFFECTIVE INDIVIDUAL."[3]
> —DR. MARK DOMBECK, AMERICAN ACADEMY OF EXPERTS IN TRAUMATIC STRESS

who experience bullying can take control of the situation by opening up to a trusted adult and finding help to make the bullying stop.

BULLYING AND SUICIDE

In regard to bullying and suicide, the Centers for Disease Control and Prevention (CDC) says, "It is correct to say that involvement in bullying, along with other risk factors, increases the chance that a young person will engage in suicide-related behaviors."[2] Unfortunately, there are many real-life stories to back up this statement. For instance, in 2010, 15-year-old Phoebe Prince died by suicide after experiencing vicious bullying from students at her school who accused her of stealing another girl's boyfriend. Five teens involved in the bullying were later arrested. They received probation and were required to do community service. In another instance, Rehtaeh Parsons, who was also 15 years old, died by suicide in 2013 after a sexually explicit photo of her getting assaulted was passed among her peers. This led to months of cyberbullying before Rehtaeh died. These are two of many examples where bullying led to suicide.

Most bullying victims do not attempt suicide. But bullying is one of several risk factors that make suicide or attempted suicide more likely. Reasons behind suicide are complex and usually include a combination of stressors. Factors including depression, trauma, and family problems contribute to suicide risk. Specific groups are also at greater risk, including Native Americans, Asian Americans, and LGBTQ youth. Lack of support from parents, schools, and peers can increase the risk, since these youth have—or feel they

WARNING SIGNS OF SUICIDE

People at risk for attempting suicide may show signs that an alert friend can spot. They may exhibit depression by showing sadness, withdrawing from people, losing interest in activities, or having trouble sleeping. They may give away favorite possessions, show reckless behavior, or undertake self-abuse or drug abuse. They may talk about death or dying, or say other things that indicate suicidal intent, such as that they can't handle life anymore or that the world would be better off without them. If someone says or does any of these things, it is important for friends to talk to the person about their concerns and get the person assistance immediately. Help can come from a counselor, doctor, or an emergency room visit. People can also reach out to the National Suicide Prevention Lifeline (1-800-273-8255) to get help.

> "BEING BULLIED CAN HAVE BOTH SHORT-TERM AND LONG-TERM EFFECTS ON A CHILD'S PSYCHOLOGICAL WELL-BEING, PHYSICAL HEALTH AND EDUCATIONAL ACHIEVEMENT."[5]
>
> —MAYO CLINIC, AN ACADEMIC AND PATIENT-SERVING HEALTH ORGANIZATION BASED IN ROCHESTER, MINNESOTA

have—no one to turn to for help. When a young person is bullied, the risk of suicide increases further still.

LONG-TERM IMPACTS

The effects of bullying can last well into adulthood. The depression and anxiety that may result from bullying can become chronic, lifelong conditions that adversely affect a person's ability to eat, sleep, work, exercise, and enjoy hobbies. They may affect the person's ability to carry out social interactions and to develop and maintain relationships.

The emotional harm caused by bullying can last much longer than the physical harm. Researchers Dieter Wolke and Suzet Tanya Lereya note, "Children who were victims of bullying have been consistently found to be at higher risk for internalizing problems, in particular diagnoses of anxiety disorder and depression in young adulthood and middle adulthood (18–50 years of age)."[4] They also say that adults who experienced bullying as children ended up with lower educational achievements, struggled more with managing finances, and earned less money than people who were not victims of bullying.

Those most affected as adults are bully-victims. These are people who have both experienced and perpetuated bullying. For example, a child might have learned how to bully when he was bullied by an abusive parent and then used this learned behavior to bully younger, smaller kids at school. Bully-victims are at a higher risk for developing childhood psychiatric disorders, panic disorders, and generalized anxiety than those who have only been victims. In addition, they have higher rates of suicide and suicidal behavior. Although researchers are not sure exactly why, something about the combination of being bullied and

THE BULLIED CHILD AS AN ADULT

Childhood experiences, including bullying, can profoundly affect people even as they enter adulthood. Childhood bullying can affect people's relationships and how they view themselves and others. Studies have found that childhood bullying had a greater effect on adult mental health than did mistreatment during adulthood. Unless bullied children or teens receive rapid and appropriate mental health treatment, they are at greater risk for a variety of mental health problems as adults. These include depression, anxiety, post-traumatic stress disorder (PTSD), self-destructive behavior, substance abuse, and suicidal thoughts and actions. They may also have difficulty developing trusting relationships.

Bullies, victims, and bully-victims are all at an elevated risk for developing mental health problems such as depression and anxiety.

then perpetuating that abuse is extremely harmful to the bully-victim.

HOW TEENS CAN STOP BULLYING

When young people are bullied or see bullying take place, how should they respond? Sometimes teens may not even realize they are being bullied. For instance, a high school junior who was a cheerleader and a member of several clubs suddenly found herself excluded from an online group chat that included most others in her social circle. A friend alerted her to videos and comments making fun of her. The online attacks became more frequent and more vicious, and the teen became isolated and very anxious at school. She feared that everyone shared this group's opinions. Only when she finally confided in her parents did she realize that she was being bullied. Intervention by her vice principal improved the situation. After the vice principal spoke with the bullies and told them how their actions could lead to suspension, the teen said she went to school "feeling protected."[6]

This girl received help from several sources. A friend let her know what was happening and helped her deal with it. The victim told her parents, who supported her and contacted her school. The vice principal acted to stop the bullying. Importantly, the bullied girl did not sit by and continue to let people's negative behavior affect her. She asked for and was given help.

Teens who are being bullied can use different tactics depending on the situation. If possible, a person can ignore the bully and leave. A bully wants his or her victim to react. But sometimes, if the victim doesn't respond the way the bully wants, the bully will lose interest. Teens can also stick close to their true friends or seek out new friends who will help defend them from bullying. In addition, teens can talk to someone they trust. This will help them deal with the anxiety and hurt that can result from bullying and increase their self-confidence. Those who observe bullying should not stay silent. It is important to tell an adult who has the power to act. This can usually be done without the bully knowing where the information came from.

Bullies might target victims whom they perceive as weak or different.

CHAPTER FOUR

WHO GETS BULLIED?

Society has various myths about who gets bullied. Perhaps the most common assumption is that bullied kids have a victim personality. That is, they are weak and did something to deserve the bullying. People may also think that bullying victims are whiners who should learn to be tougher and less sensitive. These people often think that bullying is just joking or teasing and isn't really a problem. There is also a tendency to think that only isolated kids—those with few or no friends—get bullied. All of these assumptions are incorrect, and they place the blame and the responsibility for change on the victim, rather than on the bully.

Anyone can be bullied for any reason. Bullied kids may be popular or unpopular. They may be gifted academically or not. They may be outgoing and assertive or shy. Sometimes bullying victims are different from their tormenters, belonging to a specific group that places them outside mainstream society. They may be targeted because of their race, ethnicity, religion, or because they are LGBTQ.

> "I FOUND ONE DAY IN SCHOOL A BOY OF MEDIUM SIZE ILL-TREATING A SMALLER BOY. I [EXPRESSED DISAPPROVAL], BUT HE REPLIED: 'THE BIGS HIT ME, SO I HIT THE BABIES; THAT'S FAIR.' IN THESE WORDS, HE EPITOMIZED THE HISTORY OF THE HUMAN RACE."[1]
> —PHILOSOPHER BERTRAND RUSSELL, EDUCATION AND THE SOCIAL ORDER, 1932

BULLYING TO GAIN STATUS

Bullies do not choose victims randomly. They usually target victims because demeaning them will make the bully feel better about himself or herself. For example, some bullies may be jealous of kids who excel in some area—such as sports, academics, or music—or who win prizes or receive positive attention from others. Bullies think that making their targets feel insecure or making others doubt their abilities will make the bullies feel less inferior.

Similarly, bullies may target popular or well-liked students because the bullies perceive them as a threat to their own popularity or social standing. The bully assumes that if she can diminish the popular student's likability or social standing—for example, by spreading rumors or cyberbullying—this will enhance her own standing. Such tactics can be highly damaging to the bullied teen.

BULLYING OF SPECIFIC GROUPS

Many groups that bullies target are easy to identify because they have obvious differences from the bullies. This type of bullying is usually associated with prejudice or even hatred toward those who are different. Victims of prejudicial bullying can be almost anyone. For example, they might be people with physical disabilities or body image issues. The bullying can also take any form. It may be physical, verbal, relational, digital, or some combination of these.

Bullies want to be powerful, so their targets may have certain characteristics that make them easy to manipulate and less likely to fight back. These targets may include kids who are introverted or have

PREJUDICE AND RACE

People's views about other races are influenced by family, friends, neighborhoods, and the media. People who grow up with prejudiced or racist parents may see these views as normal and acceptable when they are not. Prejudices may be based on assumptions people make when they do not know anyone of a particular race. Or they may have one encounter with a person of another race and assume all members of that race are similar. Sometimes prejudice develops because of news events. If a person of color commits a crime, a white person might wrongly assume all people of that race are criminals. However, the same white person would likely not generalize about her or his own ethnic group in the same way.

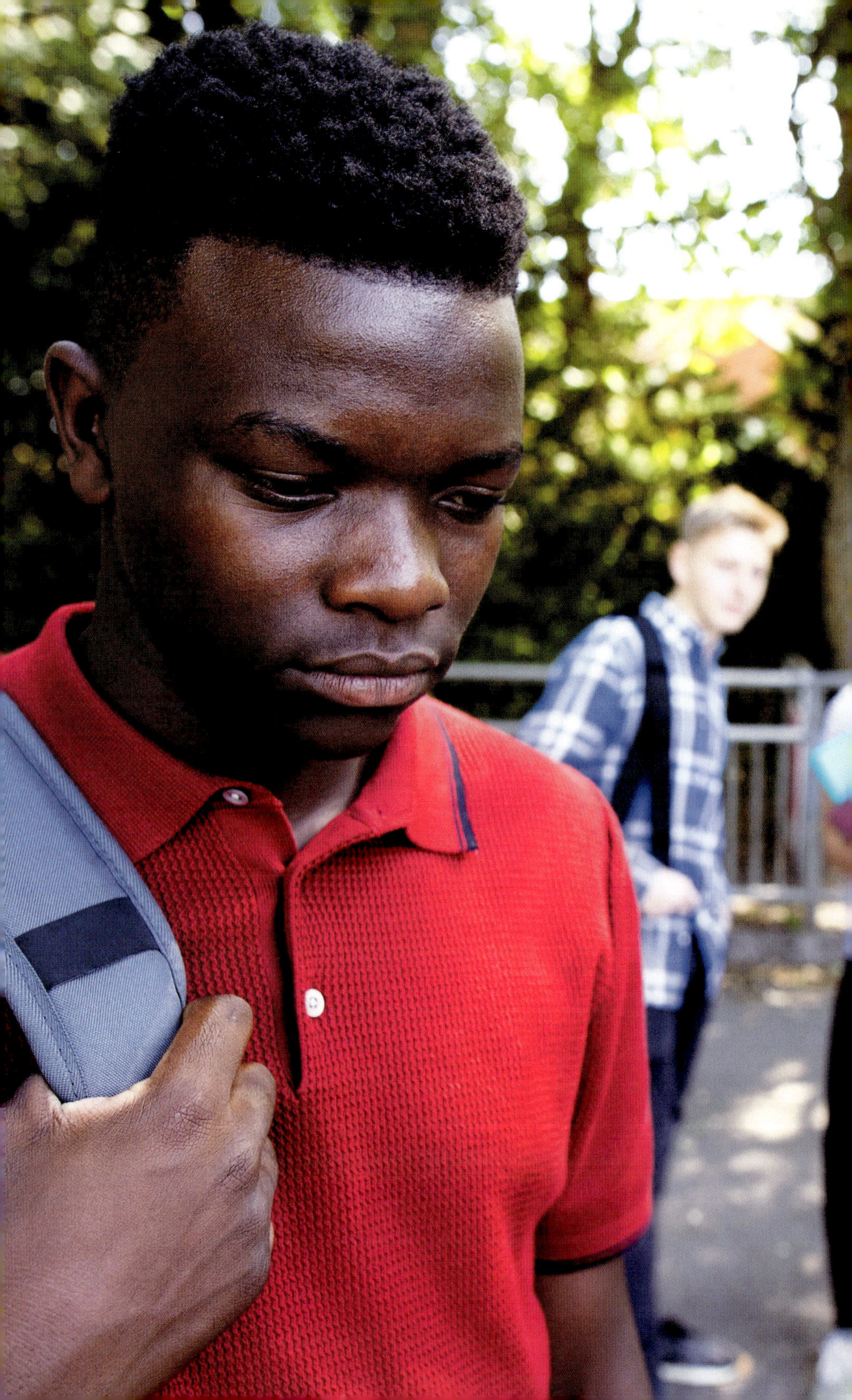

low self-esteem. They may include kids who have problems with anxiety or depression, or who are socially isolated. A person who has few friends and spends a lot of time alone makes for an easier target because it's possible people may not come to that person's aid.

Discrimination can lead to bullying of people whose race or ethnic group differs from that of the bully. Often, prejudicial bullying involves taunting, name-calling, and exclusion, but it can also escalate to physical violence, such as assault. Research suggests minority students may be at a greater risk for bullying in schools that are not diverse. For example, in a school where most students are white, Black students and other students of color may be targeted. If not stopped, prejudicial bullying can lead to hate crimes.

Religious bullying often stems from lack of knowledge or understanding about the traditions and beliefs of another religion. For example, since the September 11, 2001, terrorist attacks in the United States committed by Muslim extremists, some people have wrongly assumed that all

Prejudicial bullying is a serious issue, and legal action can be taken if it escalates.

BULLYING AS A HATE CRIME

A hate crime is a usually violent act directed at a person or group because of prejudice against the group's race, religion, sexual orientation, or some other characteristic. Childhood bullying, especially prejudicial bullying, can escalate into hate crimes. Elizabeth Englander, a professor at Bridgewater State College, suggests that one way to combat bullying in schools is to treat it as a hate crime. She designed a bullying prevention program using the same techniques involved in combating hate crimes. These techniques emphasize teaching tolerance between different groups.

Muslims are likely to be terrorists because of their religious beliefs. As a result, many Muslim students have become targets of bullying.

Bullying expert Sherri Gordon explains why people with different religious beliefs may be targeted. "Many times, religious bullying results because of preconceived ideas or a lack of understanding about the differences between religions," Gordon says. "These differences can include everything from beliefs, fasting, and prayer practices to the type of clothing they wear. Bullies point to these differences as a reason to harass and target the victim."[2]

LGBTQ individuals are often subjected to prejudicial bullying because they may be viewed as different from mainstream society. Stop Bullying, a US government

LGBTQ students are often harassed and bullied in schools just for being who they are.

website, notes LGBTQ adolescents and people who are perceived to belong to the LGBTQ community are very likely to be bullied. A 2017 survey of LGBTQ high school students across the United States found that these students were much more likely to have been bullied at school and online than their peers who identified as straight. In addition, the study found that about 10 percent of lesbian, gay, and bisexual students skipped school because they feared for their safety, as compared to 6 percent of their peers who identified as straight. Students who weren't sure of their sexual orientation were also heavily bullied, with about 24 percent of the bullying happening at school and 22 percent of it happening online.[3]

One way to counteract prejudicial bullying is to dispel the bully's ignorance. Teaching students about the cultures and practices of different racial and religious groups and teaching them to value and celebrate diversity will increase understanding. This, in turn, may help to lessen bullying.

The Equality and Human Rights Commission, a public agency in the United Kingdom, suggests several ways in which prejudicial bullying in schools can be controlled or minimized. The school should foster a whole-school culture based on safety

STATE LAWS ON BULLYING

There is no federal law on bullying. In some cases, bullying is considered a form of harassment, and schools must address it. All states, territories, and the District of Columbia have laws related to bullying, but each entity defines bullying differently and has its own set of laws and regulations. States often require schools to set up bullying policies, including procedures they should follow to investigate and respond to bullying incidents. A few states require bullying prevention programs or make bullying prevention part of their health education standards. But most state laws do not include consequences for bullying, and few classify it as a criminal offense.

and inclusivity. This requires taking every report of bullying seriously and having a good reporting system so that bullying is identified when it occurs. Schools should not blame the victim or expect the person to adjust his or her behaviors. The responsibility to adjust behaviors lies with the bully. Schools should strive to make sure all bullies are identified. Changing the group attitude can help improve the situation too. School officials should monitor prejudice and prejudicial bullying in the school, listen to students, and learn from previous incidents.

A PUBLIC HEALTH ISSUE

Many people view bullying as a serious public health issue because of its dangerous and long-lasting effects. In 2016, the National Academies of Sciences, Engineering, and Medicine published a report linking bullying to a variety of physical and emotional health issues. In addition, the report noted that

> "WE NEED TO UNDERSTAND THAT [BULLYING] IS A PUBLIC HEALTH PROBLEM. . . . IT HAS A MAJOR EFFECT ON [CHILDREN'S] ACADEMIC PERFORMANCE AS WELL AS THEIR MENTAL AND PHYSICAL HEALTH."[4]
>
> —DR. FREDERICK RIVARA, CHAIR OF A COMMITTEE COMPILING THE 2016 REPORT ON BULLYING BY THE NATIONAL ACADEMIES OF SCIENCES, ENGINEERING, AND MEDICINE

PBIS AND SEL

Two evidence-based methods of dealing with bullying in schools are Positive Behavioral Interventions and Supports (PBIS) and Social and Emotional Learning (SEL). PBIS emphasizes a teacher-centered approach based on the study of applied behavior. It involves teaching and modeling desired behaviors and using positive reinforcement techniques to manage behaviors and prevent problems. Students are given rules for appropriate behavior and are taught to follow them. Examples of such rules include: be safe, be respectful, and be responsible.

SEL is a more student-centered approach. It teaches students the skills needed to control their own actions. They may receive short lessons in understanding their feelings and the feelings of others, dealing with anger, thinking clearly, and solving social problems. Both PBIS and SEL use positive approaches rather than punishments. And both emphasize teaching skills that will ensure students' success.

bullying changes the stress-response system in bullies and in their victims. These changes impair cognitive functions and the ability to regulate emotions. Both bullies and victims are more likely to be depressed and consider or attempt suicide. They show increased risk of substance abuse as adults, and they may engage in high-risk activities including theft and vandalism.

Dr. Catherine P. Bradshaw is a professor at the University of Virginia. She recommends a three-tiered public health approach for preventing bullying. This approach begins with universal programs aimed at all students. Programs should be designed to improve school climate, address bystander behavior, and clarify the school's rules about acceptable behaviors. Students who do not respond completely to universal programs may be targeted with more selective programs. Training in social skills and emotional control may be provided for students who are likely to become involved in bullying. The most extreme interventions are reserved for the students who are already showing signs of problem behaviors. These interventions are usually tailored to the individual student. They may include mental and behavioral health treatments and often involve the student's family.

Bullies tend to be more powerful than their victims, either in physical size or social status.

CHAPTER FIVE

WHY DOES BULLYING HAPPEN?

All types of people are bullied, and all types of people can be bullies. But there are risk factors related to personality, behavior, and family life that make people more likely to become bullies. Also, some life situations cause people to experience jealousy, seek power and popularity, or want revenge. All of these may lead to bullying. The reasons behind what makes a bully are complex, and they are dependent on the situation.

RISK FACTORS

Certain character traits seem to occur in kids and teens who become bullies, such as being more assertive or aggressive. Bullying others can give them a sense of power and control, at least for a while. Some may already have control, but they want more. This is true, for example, of popular kids, successful athletes, or people who are already large, strong, and aggressive.

TEACHING IMPORTANT EMOTIONAL SKILLS

Empathy is an important emotion for people to have in order to be successful in life. Children can learn empathy from their parents. Kids can also learn how to cope with negative emotions, such as jealousy and anger, by watching and listening to their parents and through problem-solving rather than bullying. When a child does something hurtful, a parent can ask, "How would you feel if . . . ?"[1] This forces the child to consider the situation from the other's point of view. Adults can also teach children to name emotions, both positive and negative, and discuss the emotions they see around them in everyday life and in media.

Teens may seek to maintain or enhance their own popularity by demeaning others. They may even brag about their bullying exploits to attract attention.

People who lack empathy are more likely to become bullies. They either don't understand or don't care that their actions are cruel or painful to others. They might even blame the person they are bullying, saying it's the victim's fault for being weak or not being able to take teasing.

Physical factors can lead to bullying as well. One of the most common is using greater size and strength to bully and overpower others. Combined with aggression, this can be one way to gain and keep control. Aggressive kids may have poor impulse control and might be unable or unwilling to use verbal skills or reasoning to interact with others.

They may also exclude certain kids from a group and encourage group members to exclude them as well.

Would-be bullies have a tendency to react negatively to people around them and show intolerance to anyone who is different, which may lead to prejudicial bullying. They also might have difficulty handling frustration, and rather than practice patience, they use force to get their way.

The tendency to bully may be increased when children or teens see or experience bullying themselves, perhaps by a parent or sibling. Anger and violence within the family can be learned, and children then turn this learned behavior on others—typically younger, smaller kids—outside the home. Finally, permissive parents who fail to set rules or consequences for negative actions may also be a risk factor when it comes to their children developing bullying behavior.

> "NOBODY . . . HAS EXPLAINED TO [BULLIES] WHAT IT MEANS TO HURT ANOTHER PERSON'S FEELINGS. . . . [SUCH PEOPLE ARE] IMPAIRED IN THEIR ABILITY TO PERCEIVE ANOTHER PERSON'S DISTRESS."[2]
>
> —DENIS SUKHODOLSKY, PhD, EXPERT IN ANGER AND AGGRESSION IN CHILDREN

Bullies may have extreme physical reactions to frustration or other negative emotions.

WHY PEOPLE BECOME BULLIES

In some cases, rather than seeking power, bullies are simply bowing to peer pressure to fit in with the group. These bullies may know it is wrong, but they do it anyway because others in the group are doing it.

Some people think pushing others around is fun or entertaining. Such people lack empathy; they do not recognize the harm and hurt they are causing. Those who don't have empathy often engage in prejudicial bullying.

They have no tolerance for diversity and bully anyone who is different from them. And bully-victims often lash out to either get revenge on those who have bullied them or to make someone else feel the pain that they do.

Relational aggression is often rooted in jealousy. For example, if a girl is insecure about her own worth, she may compare herself to others and feel that she fails to measure up. She feels inadequate compared to those against whom she is measuring herself. This is especially true when she looks at social media, where people tend to post only about their successes. The girl becomes envious, and she may retaliate by bullying those of whom she is jealous.

In situations involving direct competition, such as sports, bullying may be used as a method to diminish or eliminate the competition. A bully may attempt to raise her own status by lowering the status of a competitor.

BULLYING ROLES

Participants in bullying fall into five roles: bully, victim, assistant, defender, and outsider. Assistants help the bully harass the victim. Defenders and outsiders are bystanders. Defenders help the victim and often have strong social skills. Their behavior helps victims and may help bullies learn empathy. Outsiders don't take part in either the bullying or helping the victim. Outsiders may suffer negative effects from bullying just by watching.

MEAN THINGS BULLIES SAY

In verbal bullying, the bully may try to downplay what he or she said. The bully is refusing to accept responsibility for the hurtful words. One common phrase a bully might say is "my bad." In this case, the bully is admitting he said something hurtful without apologizing for it. Another thing he or she might say is "chill out," which suggests the victim is overreacting and implies that the victim's feelings are not valid. "I'm sorry, but . . ." is another commonly used phrase. The word *but* turns an apology into a nonapology. Whatever comes after "but" turns the blame on the victim and says "you deserved it." A person might also follow up his or her verbal bullying with "just kidding" or "no offense."[3] These are usually phrases that either follow or precede hurtful words that the bully is not owning up to.

PUTTING A STOP TO BULLYING

Often teens can feel powerless when bullying happens. They should always tell adults—both parents and teachers—when they see bullying taking place or are bullied themselves. But there are also things teens can do to protect themselves and the people around them. Most importantly, people should always treat others with respect and avoid any type of bullying behavior themselves. If they end up hurting someone they should apologize immediately and sincerely.

At school, teens who are bullied can avoid places where bullying occurs. They should also stay near an adult

Bullies may spread rumors about those whom they feel threatened by or jealous of in order to damage their victims' reputations.

if possible. This deters bullies from attacking their victims, because they don't want to face negative repercussions from an adult.

If someone is the victim of bullying, it's important for the person to stay calm, ignore the bully, and walk away. Bullies are looking for a reaction from the victim. By not responding to the bully, it's possible that the bully will get the message that a person doesn't care what the bully says and can't be intimidated. The US government website Stop Bullying also has tips on how to handle a situation like this: "Look at the kid bullying you and tell him or her to stop in

WHY TEENS CYBERBULLY

Some reasons for cyberbullying are similar to the reasons for any other type of bullying. Kids seek power or want to improve their social status, they lack empathy, they think all their friends are doing it and they want to fit in, or they are just bored. But because it is online, cyberbullying is somewhat different from traditional bullying. The bully does not see his or her victims and therefore is less likely to feel remorse for causing them pain. Often, people cyberbully because they want to cause pain. They may be seeking revenge because they, too, have been bullied. They might think the victim deserves to be bullied because of some real or imagined slight against the bully. And because cyberbullying can be anonymous, the bully feels safe and is unlikely to get caught.

a calm, clear voice. You can also try to laugh it off. This works best if joking is easy for you. It could catch the kid bullying you off guard."[4] However, sometimes people don't feel comfortable standing up to the bully in this way. Stop Bullying says, "If speaking up seems too hard or not safe, walk away and stay away. Don't fight back. Find an adult to stop the bullying on the spot."[5]

Bystanders can help stop bullying too. They can stand up for people who are being tormented by another person and also befriend the victim. This will let bullies know that their victims have allies, and they will be less likely to target them.

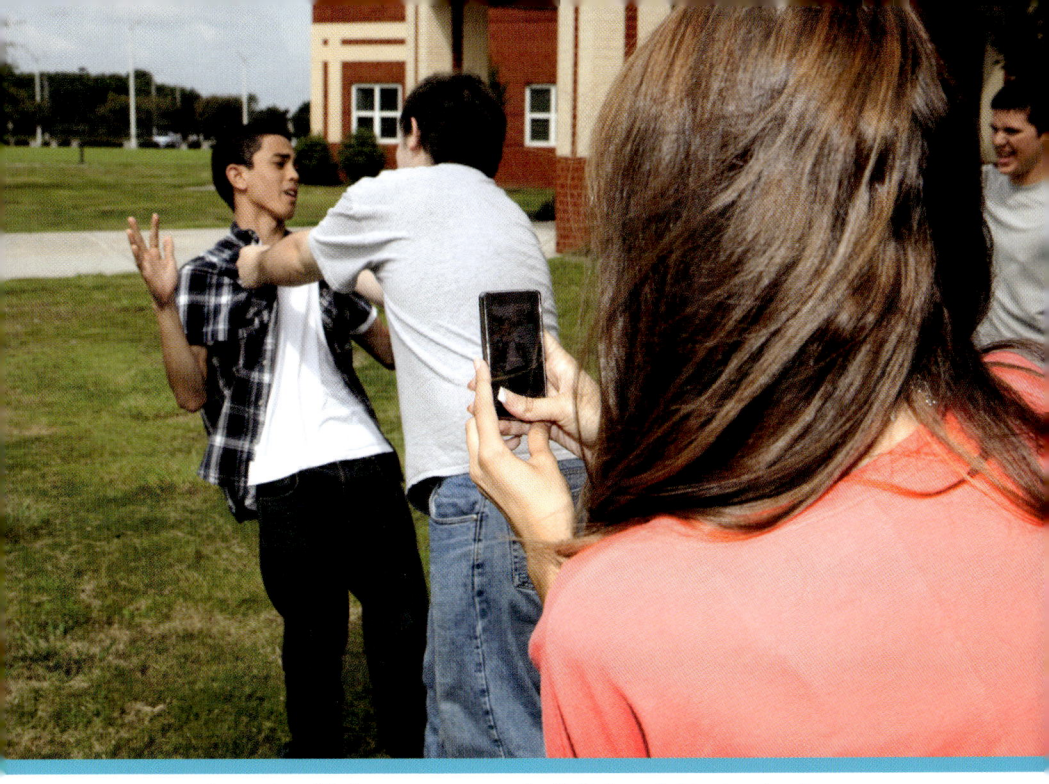

Bystanders shouldn't encourage a bully's hurtful behavior by giving the bully an audience. Instead, they should find a way to help the victim.

The reasons for bullying are complex and sometimes difficult to determine. But it is important to remember that the fault lies with the bully, not the victim, and that the bully has problems that cause the poor behavior. He or she needs help and understanding, as well.

> "WHEN CULTURES CONDONE AND IN SOME CASES CELEBRATE VIOLENCE AND AGGRESSION . . . THEY UNWITTINGLY GIVE LICENSE TO AND ENCOURAGE BULLIES."[6]
>
> —DR. HOGAN SHERROW, EVOLUTIONARY ANTHROPOLOGIST, OHIO UNIVERSITY

Tom Brown's Schooldays had images of children fighting in its 1911 edition.

CHAPTER SIX

A HISTORY OF BULLYING

Serious research on bullying did not begin until the 1980s. However, bullying has been recognized as a problem and written about since at least the mid-1800s. A famous book, *Tom Brown's Schooldays*, first published in 1857, gives this example: "'Very well then, let's roast him,' cried Flashman, and catches hold of Tom by the collar: one or two boys hesitate, but the rest join in."[1] The preface to the sixth edition of this popular book includes a letter from a school friend of the author, which clearly describes the harm that can result from bullying. At the time, people recognized that bullying occurred routinely in group situations such as schools, camps, barracks, and ship's crews, and that it involved boys or men. One incident was described in an 1862 article in the *Times* of London, England, which reported the death of a soldier due to bullying.

BULLYING AROUND THE WORLD

According to Richard Donegan of Elon University, bullying is a survival tactic. It has been used by humans in order to compete for limited resources. Donegan notes that in the United States, the capitalistic society has led to competition in which success is measured by a person's wealth, and bullying to achieve this goal is ingrained at a young age. Children are taught to be the best they can be, and they quickly learn ways to get ahead in school and life—many of which involve bullying tactics.

> "THE BULLYING PROPENSITIES OF HUMAN NATURE HAVE . . . THESE REMARKABLE CHARACTERISTICS THAT . . . THEY SETTLE UPON SOME ONE OBJECT AND STICK CLOSE AND FAITHFULLY AND PERSEVERINGLY TO IT. THEY ARE ABOUT THE MOST UNCHANGEABLE THING THAT THIS FICKLE WORLD POSSESSES."[2]
> —*THE TIMES (LONDON), AUGUST 6, 1862*

The development of technology has furthered bullying tools. The rise in number of cell phones and in social media use enables kids to communicate much more, but it also makes them more vulnerable, as social media presents sides of them that were traditionally kept private. It gives bullies another platform to perform their negative behaviors.

Bullying does not look the same everywhere. Its patterns differ depending on the culture in which it occurs. Hyojin Koo of Woosuk University in South Korea describes the history of bullying in the United Kingdom, Japan, and Korea. In the United Kingdom in the 1800s, the term *bullying* was seldom used. This type of behavior was usually described as "everyday violence" or "interpersonal violence," and it was considered routine.[3] It happened among both children and adults and often involved power differences. Immigrants, such as the Irish, and people who spoke different languages were bullied. Bullying was common in institutions and in schools,

COMPETITIVE BULLYING

Richard Donegan of Elon University suggests that problems of bullying and cyberbullying in the United States stem from an intensely competitive modern society. Bullying, Donegan says, has been ingrained in US society since its founding and has remained a problem throughout its history. Examples in today's world include the win-at-all-costs attitude in sports and other ventures, the highly competitive college admission process, and the business world. Cyberbullying has increased the problem, allowing the bully to remain anonymous and avoid directly confronting victims. This can make the bullying crueler than if it were face-to-face. Donegan describes two bullying control methods—prevention programs and laws—but cautions that, because society and especially technology will continue to evolve, methods of bullying control must evolve with them.

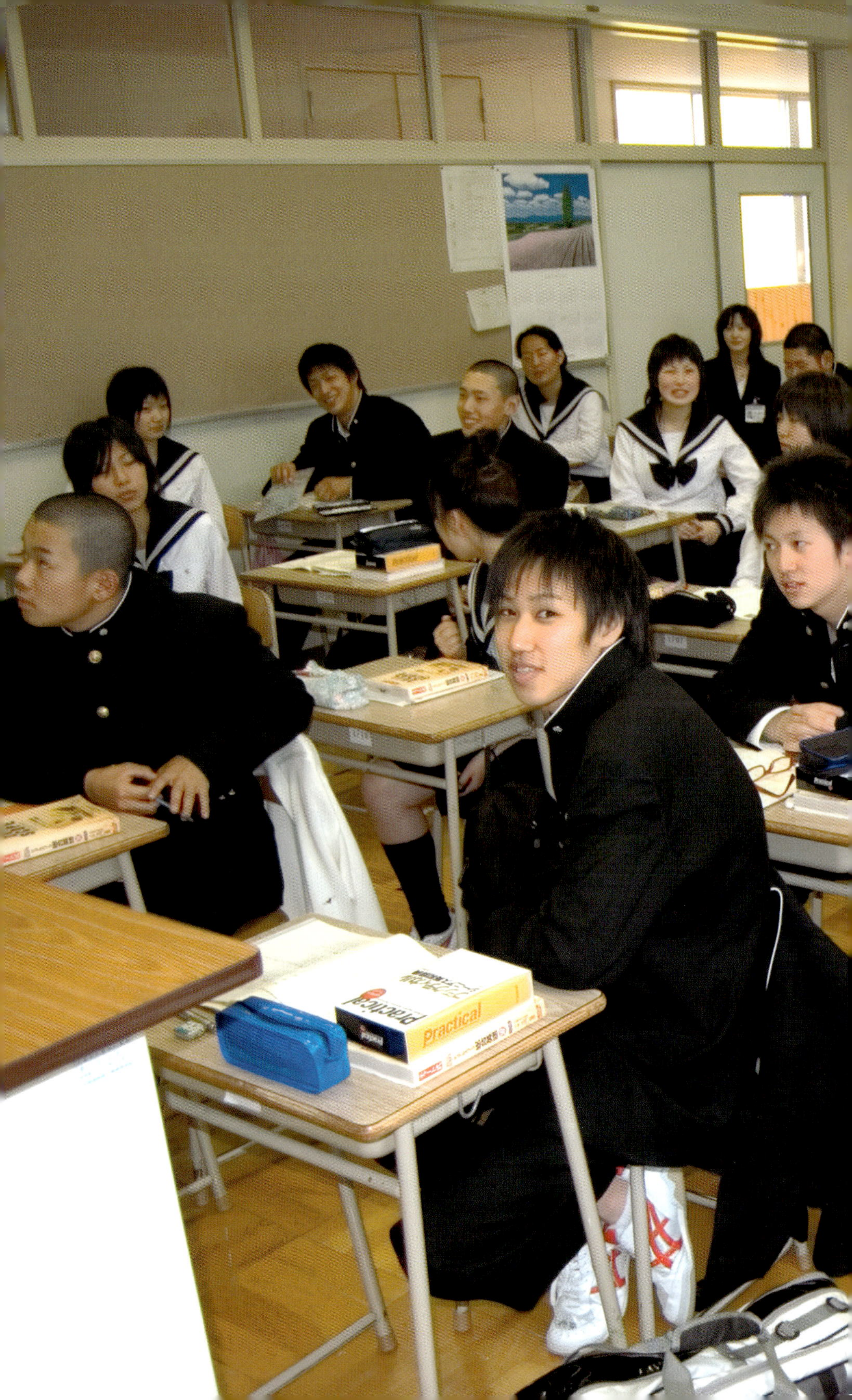
Practical

as described in *Tom Brown's Schooldays*. At that time, bullying was described almost entirely in terms of physical violence.

Bullying in Japan is very different. It is known as *ijime*, and in the 1600s through the 1800s, it often occurred in a family context. Parents punished children with short periods of isolation, separation from family, and threats of abandonment. Although ijime has existed for many years, it only became recognized as a problem in the 1970s. Whereas school bullying in many cultures tends to involve older students harassing younger ones, in Japan, it usually occurs among children in the same grade. Whether at home or at school, ijime uses psychological harm—primarily ostracism. In addition to loneliness, ostracism causes great shame in a society where conformity and acceptance are highly valued.

The history of bullying in Korea has involved both psychological and physical assaults. For instance, in the Choson Dynasty, which began in 1392, bullying and hazing was used by senior officers as a method of welcoming junior officers.

In 2018, bullying in Japanese schools reached a record high.

The junior officer was isolated and ostracized by all senior officers, and he was not told of required events, causing him to be punished for missing them. There was physical harassment as well. The intent was to make the victim feel shame, which was viewed as a fate as severe as death in some classes of Korean culture. The treatment was meant to last a week or two, but in some cases it lasted for a year or more and led some victims to die by suicide. This form of bullying had all the major characteristics accepted in today's definition: intent to cause harm, a power imbalance, and behavior that was repeated over a long time period.

A CHANGING DEFINITION

The term *bully* has been around since 1530, but it began as a positive term. It likely came from the Dutch word for "brother" or "lover." However, the term later became synonymous with *ruffian*, which was defined in the 1530s as "a boisterous, brutal fellow, one ready to commit any crime." In 1710, *bully* as a verb was defined as to "overbear with bluster or menaces." In 1777, the noun *bullying* meant "insolent tyrannizing, personal intimidation"—close to the present-day meaning of the word.[4]

RESEARCH ON BULLYING

According to Koo, World War II (1939–1945) led to an increased concern about bullying, as the atrocities of the war opened people's eyes to questions of human dignity and rights. A United Nations document published in 1948 stressed the right of humans to be free from the threat of violence, stating that "everyone has the right to life, liberty, and security of person."[5] Earlier wars generated these concerns as well, but the widespread increase in press coverage made World War II more influential.

In 1978, Dan Olweus conducted the first systematic study on bullying. In his earliest study, he limited his definition of bullying to physical violence and did not include indirect bullying. Later studies in the 1980s and 1990s included girls as participants in bullying, and they added verbal and psychological threats as part of his definition. Olweus described bullying as "a subset of aggressive behavior, characterized by repetition and an imbalance of power."[6]

Much of the research during the decades of the 1980s and 1990s centered around developing a more precise and

WORKPLACE BULLYING

Bullying occurs in the workplace as well as in schools. In the 1980s, Swedish psychologist Heinz Leymann analyzed bullying that occurred at work. In the early 1990s, British journalist Andrea Adams did a series of documentaries that popularized the term *workplace bullying*. While control and prevention of bullying in the United States first became an issue in schools and government agencies, more US researchers in the 1990s began to study psychologically abusive behavior in the workplace. Businesses became concerned because of its negative effect on their profits.

complete definition of bullying. A series of national reports published around 1999 showed that bullying existed in very similar forms in many countries around the world, including the United States, Canada, Japan, Australia, New Zealand, and various developing countries.

Modern definitions of bullying cover the same characteristics. Sonia Sharp and Peter K. Smith, editors of a 1994 book summarizing contemporary research on school bullying, define it as "a systematic abuse of power."[7] It is generally considered repetitive, and it is assumed that victims are unable to defend themselves. These characteristics have been summarized by Koo into the four Ps: power, pain, persistence, and premeditation. The word *power* indicates the imbalance of power in the bully and victim relationship; the bully can engage in physical or psychological violence

> "NO MATTER WHERE YOU GO IN THE WORLD, FROM THE MBUTI OF CENTRAL AFRICA . . . TO SUBURBAN CHILDREN IN THE UNITED STATES . . . THERE ARE INDIVIDUALS AND GROUPS THAT TARGET OTHERS WITH TACTICS DESIGNED TO INTIMIDATE, COERCE OR HARM THEM. . . . BULLYING, IT SEEMS, IS PART OF OUR NORMAL BEHAVIORAL REPERTOIRE; IT IS PART OF THE HUMAN CONDITION."[8]
>
> —DR. HOGAN SHERROW, EVOLUTIONARY ANTHROPOLOGIST, OHIO UNIVERSITY

School policies in much of the United States today have a strict stance on bullying and do not tolerate discrimination. Teachers work to promote a safe learning environment.

that the victim cannot counteract. *Pain* specifies the stress, anxiety, and other health problems that the victim suffers, even when the bully is not present. In the worst cases, pain may lead to suicide. *Persistence* indicates constant repetition of the bullying behavior. *Premeditation* stresses the bully's intention to cause harm.

Today, the definition of bullying includes verbal and emotional abuse, as well as physical violence and cyberbullying. Bullying was once seen as a part of growing up, something kids had to live through. Now, it is seen as a social problem that needs to be controlled and prevented.

People can talk with their friends and come up with ideas on how to stop bullying if they see it.

CHAPTER SEVEN

THE BULLY AND THE BYSTANDER

According to the US government website Stop Bullying, "Someone who witnesses bullying, either in person or online, is a bystander. Friends, students, peers, teachers, school staff, parents, coaches, and other youth-serving adults can be bystanders. With cyberbullying, even strangers can be bystanders."[1] Research shows that most cases of bullying are witnessed by other people. It also shows that when people intervene and try to stop bullying, the negative behavior of the bully stops within ten seconds approximately one-half of the time.[2] Bystanders can make a difference.

By being present during bullying and doing nothing, bystanders become part of the bullying. And while numerous students know about bullying, many incidents are unreported. Debra Pepler of York University notes that about 85 percent of bullying incidents have student witnesses. In addition, witnesses participate in the bullying about 75 percent of the time. Approximately

> "STUDENTS WHO EXPERIENCE BULLYING ARE MORE LIKELY TO FIND PEER ACTIONS HELPFUL THAN EDUCATOR OR SELF-ACTIONS."[5]
> —*PACER'S NATIONAL BULLYING PREVENTION CENTER*

50 percent of students assume that, even if they did report bullying, nothing would be done.[3] Also, secrecy is a part of the bullying culture. Bullies often impose a code of silence by threatening others with retaliation if they tell. Thus, any student—victim or bystander—who reports a bully is taking a risk, and most choose not to.

THE BULLY

According to *Psychology Today*, "Bullies are made, not born, and it happens at an early age; if the normal aggression of 2-year-olds is not handled with consistency, children fail to acquire internal restraints against such behavior."[4] Research indicates that bullying peaks around ages 11 to 13—the middle school years. Middle school students tend to rely more on physical bullying such as kicking, hitting, and shoving. As they mature into teens, the form of bullying tends more toward relational aggression, such as ostracism and spreading rumors.

The aggressive, often cruel behavior displayed by bullies makes it easy to be concerned only with the effects of bullying on the target or victim. But bullying has lifelong effects on the bully, as well. Preventing bullying and redirecting the bullies' actions into more positive channels will help both victims and bullies have happier lives and decrease the likelihood that bullying will continue in the future.

A 2013 study in *JAMA Psychiatry* involved 1,400 kids ages nine to 16, with follow-ups done until age 26.[6] The group included bullies, victims, and bully-victims. All three groups showed an increased risk for psychological problems including depression; anxiety; panic disorders; agoraphobia, which is fear of open spaces or crowds; and suicidal thinking or behavior.

NARCISSISTIC BULLYING

Narcissists are people who think only of themselves. They respond to every situation as though its only importance is how it affects them. When narcissists are also bullies, they may relate to others by means of narcissistic monologuing. That means they will monopolize every conversation by being louder and more aggressive than everyone else. When others try to speak, narcissists cut them off or drown them out. They refuse to listen to others and do not abide by the give-and-take rules of normal conversation. They want control and attention and feel they are more entitled to speak than anyone else. Experts such as author Julie L. Hall suggest that people avoid narcissists and cut them out of their lives if possible.

People who drop out of high school don't have as many job opportunities and have lower salaries on average than their peers who graduate.

Bullies drop out of school more frequently than others, and they tend to begin sexual activity earlier. In the *JAMA Psychiatry* study, psychological problems were still evident at age 26. Bullies were four to five times more likely to suffer from antisocial personality disorder, which is characterized by lying, a lack of empathy, and often criminal behavior.[7]

Psychology Today notes that if bullies do not learn to overcome their actions, they may grow into antisocial adults who abuse their spouses and children and produce another generation of bullies. Adult bullies have trouble keeping jobs, forming and maintaining relationships, and using drugs and alcohol responsibly. They are more likely to have criminal records and to carry weapons. By their mid-twenties, they have more traffic violations and exhibit four times as much criminal behavior as their peers. And by their mid-thirties, 60 percent of former middle school bullies have at least one criminal conviction.[8] Bully-victims are at the highest risk for psychological problems as adults. They are five times more likely to develop depression and ten to 25 times more likely to develop anxiety compared to those not involved in bullying incidents.[9]

THE BYSTANDER

Some bullies seek out their victims in isolated places, such as the bathroom or a deserted hallway. But when bullies

TATTLING VS. TELLING

Sometimes students resist reporting incidents of bullying to avoid being labeled tattletales or snitches. But bullying is serious and potentially dangerous, and students need to be reassured that they should tell an adult it is happening. They should understand the difference between tattling and telling. Tattling is telling on someone merely to get them in trouble. Telling is getting help from an adult to stop someone from being hurt or to protect someone's right to be safe and free from fear and harm. Students should know that adults will respect them and take them seriously, and that bullies have less power than they seem to. They should understand that most people do not like bullying and want it to stop.

want an audience, bullying occurs in plain sight, such as in the cafeteria, in the schoolyard, in the hallways between classes, or on the bus. When there are bystanders to a bullying incident, often they do not intervene. They may even participate in the bullying or egg on the bully. They may not want to be seen as tattletales, or they may fear being associated with the victim, either because the bully might retaliate or because they worry that intervening will lower their own social status. Bystanders may feel uncomfortable, guilty, and helpless in the presence of bullying.

But while bystanders often feel as though their intervention would have no effect, students being bullied welcome help from bystanders. Actions they considered most helpful included spending time with the bullied person, calling or talking to them, helping them get away, telling an adult or helping them tell an adult, or confronting the bully.

According to marriage and family therapist Ann Steele, bystanders should recognize that their decision not to intervene is not a passive action. This decision is harmful to the victim and to themselves. Bystanders of bullying who do not intervene are more likely than defenders to smoke and drink, skip school, and suffer from depression and anxiety. These factors carry over into adulthood in bystanders, just as they do in those more directly involved in bullying.

THE BYSTANDER INTERVENTION MODEL

In 1970, psychologists John Darley and Bibb Latané noted that there are five steps a bystander takes when intervening in a bullying incident. First, the bystander must notice the event. Then, he or she must interpret it as an emergency requiring help. The bystander needs to accept responsibility for intervening and also know how to intervene or help. The last step is to act.

Defenders, or bystanders who help, have several characteristics not found in outsiders, or those who don't help. They are more likely to be girls and are likely to interpret a situation as an emergency. They feel a greater sense of responsibility to intervene, and they have a greater knowledge of how to intervene.

Comforting and befriending a victim can have a great effect on a victim's emotional health. It may also deter bullies from targeting the victim again.

INTERRUPTING BULLYING

It is important to stop episodes of bullying when they occur. But if they continue to happen over and over—as bullying does when unchecked—the school has a bullying culture, and that culture needs to be interrupted and turned around. If teachers and students are tolerant of bullying, it will continue to thrive. But if they promote a school culture that is respectful, humane, and tolerant of all people, there will be less of a place for bullying.

The process of transforming a school must involve everyone who works and goes to the school. The school must develop policies and strategies for bullying prevention that involve all aspects of school life and all members of the community—students, teachers, administrators, and parents. Each group must have the resources and training it needs to succeed. School bullying is a form of aggression and results in abuse. Thus, a key part of interrupting bullying must be

SOME WAYS TO PREVENT BULLYING

The methods each school uses to promote a culture of inclusion and respect will vary, but some general guidelines are appropriate anywhere. These include recognizing and validating the individual abilities and value of each person and recognizing and promoting diversity. Schools can also help students get involved in problem-solving and decision-making about issues of importance to them, including bullying. Ensuring that students' concerns are heard and taken seriously is also important, as is ensuring the school promotes empathy and focuses on the rights and responsibilities of all. Schools should also involve parents and community members and model the type of behavior desired in the school at all times.

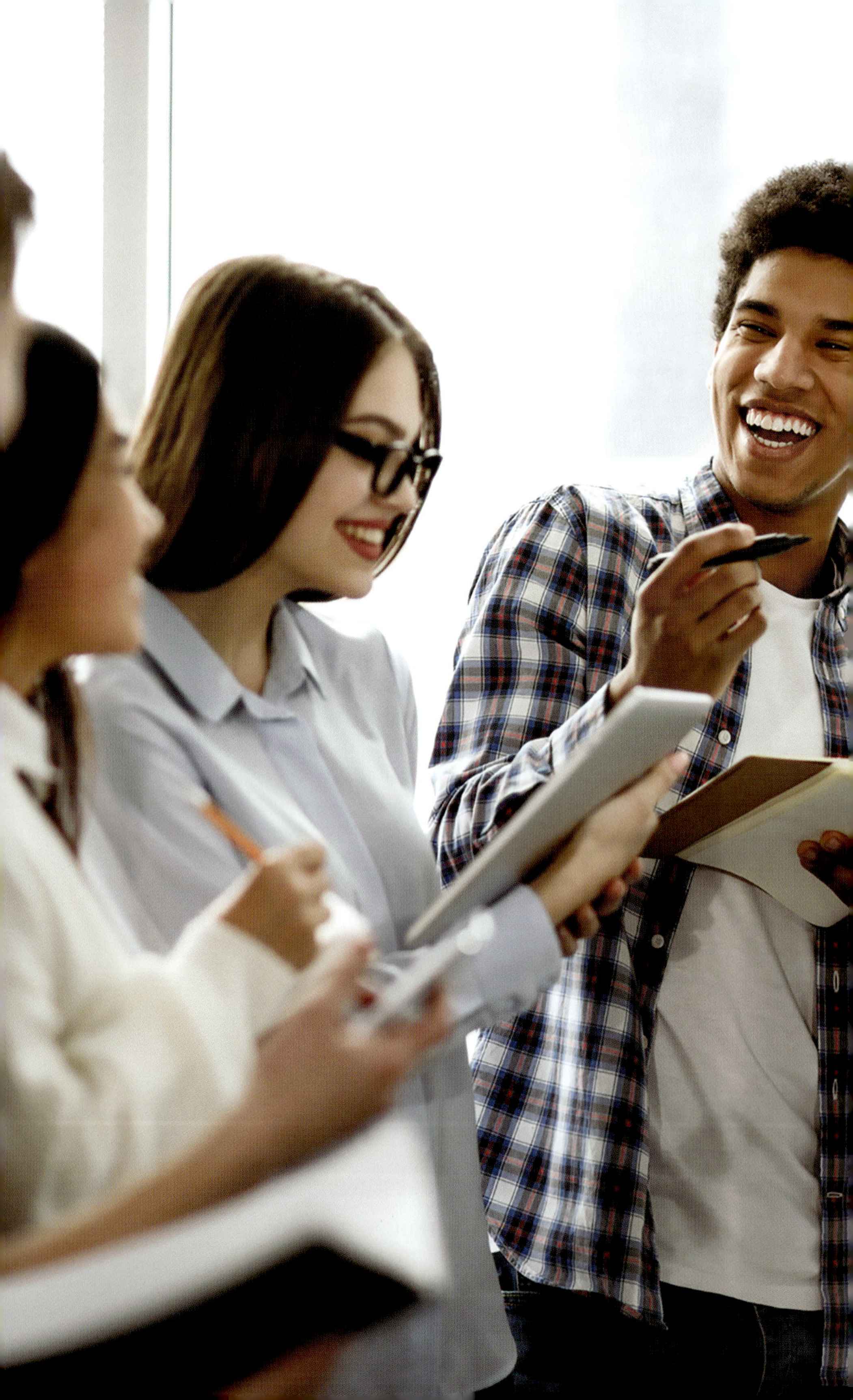

teaching young people that aggression and violence are never acceptable. This means dealing directly with common social inequities that trigger bullying, including racism, sexism, homophobia, religious bigotry, and discrimination against people with disabilities.

> "IF WE DON'T INVOLVE BYSTANDERS, WE CAN'T SOLVE THE PROBLEM. . . . YOU ALSO CAN HAVE ISOLATION IN THE MIDDLE OF A CAFETERIA IF A BULLY CONVINCES EVERYBODY ELSE NOT TO INTERVENE. . . . IF WE CAN SHOW BYSTANDERS HOW TO BECOME INVOLVED AS BYSTANDERS, WE REDUCE ISOLATION."[10]
>
> —RICHARD HAZLER, PROFESSOR OF COUNSELOR EDUCATION, OHIO UNIVERSITY

Many antibullying organizations think it should be a school policy that discrimination and mistreatment based on these issues should not be tolerated.

By working together, students and school officials can create a safe, supportive educational environment.

Bystanders can ask a person who is being bullied what they can do to help.

CHAPTER EIGHT

OVERCOMING BULLYING

Much of the research on bullying as a social problem has revolved around developing a more precise definition of bullying and analyzing when and where it occurs. But another important branch of research deals with how to tackle the problem of bullying and what schools, parents, and teens themselves can do to prevent or decrease bullying.

A SCHOOL ANTIBULLYING PROGRAM

Antibullying programs are being developed by schools more and more often as the problem of bullying receives more attention. One antibullying program is the Olweus Bullying Prevention Program (OBPP). It was founded by Dan Olweus, the researcher who did pioneering work on bullying. OBPP has been successfully implemented throughout the world. It is designed for students five to 15 years old and can be adapted for use with older students too. It is designed to make schools safer and more positive places.

School staff members may work with students to learn more about bullying situations in their schools. More information will help them make progress in stopping bullying.

    The ultimate goals of OBPP include reducing existing bullying problems, preventing the development of new bullying problems, and improving peer relationships at school. These goals are accomplished by restructuring the academic environment to reduce opportunities for bullying and to build a sense of community within the school. Adults participating in the program are asked to follow four key principles. First, show warmth and positive interest toward students. Second, set firm limits on unacceptable behavior. Third, when rules are broken, respond with consistent, nonhostile, nonphysical negative consequences. Fourth, function as authorities and positive role models.

The program's components include school-wide, classroom, and individual elements. At the school level, a committee is appointed to coordinate the bullying program. Training is carried out for members of the committee and all school staff. The Olweus Bully/Victim Questionnaire about bullying is administered to all students. This screening determines the extent of the problem and serves as a baseline to monitor progress. Then, the school's rules against bullying (designed by each school) are introduced. The staff holds periodic meetings to monitor progress.

WHAT DOESN'T WORK

Certain policies used to control bullying in some schools are ineffective. It does not help to put bullies and victims together to work out their differences with staff as mediators. The victim will still be intimidated, and the bullying will continue after the mediation. Telling students to report bullying may not work in middle and high schools. Students may be afraid to report bullying, or they may not trust teachers or administrators. Although bullying should not be tolerated, a too strict no-tolerance policy can sometimes lead to overreaction, in which simple teasing is treated as bullying. Finally, if teachers or administrators intimidate students, they are unlikely to develop an antibullying school culture.

THE OLWEUS BULLY/VICTIM QUESTIONNAIRE

An important part of the OBPP is the Bully/Victim Questionnaire. This questionnaire has been updated periodically since its development in 1996. It has multiple-choice questions for children about their school life for the several months prior to answering the questionnaire. It is designed to learn how much and what kind of bullying is occurring, as well as how the person has responded. The questionnaire is administered when the OBPP first begins and at intervals thereafter to gauge the program's effectiveness. A sample question is: "Have you been bullied at school in the past couple of months in one or more of the following ways? Please answer all questions." This is followed by a series of choices, including "I was called mean names" and "Other students left me out of things on purpose."[1]

At the classroom level, teachers post and enforce the school's antibullying rules. They hold weekly class meetings to discuss bullying-related topics. At the individual level, school staff members monitor student activities in and out of the classroom, and they intervene immediately when a bullying incident occurs. They meet separately with the bully, the victim, and parents. If necessary, they develop individualized programs for students to help them better understand and follow the school rules.

A thorough assessment of OBPP outcomes was done in

Norway between 2001 and 2006. About 3,000 students in grades four to seven were followed for five years. During this time, the overall rate of being bullied decreased by about 40 percent and the rate of bullying others decreased by about 51 percent. Olweus found these results encouraging because they suggested that schools had made positive changes in their cultures. Students in grades eight to ten showed smaller improvements (about a 32 percent decrease in bullied students) and more variable results, suggesting that achieving positive results in older students might take longer.[2]

A 2016 article by the Hazelden Foundation indicated that OBPP led to significant reductions in antisocial behavior, including not only bullying but also school violence, fighting, and truancy. Studies showed improvements in classroom climate, such as better discipline, more positive social relationships, better support for bully-victims, and more effective intervention for bullies themselves.

WHAT PARENTS CAN DO

A 2017 study by Australian experts including Leanne Lester and her colleagues indicates that involving parents and families is essential to the success of school antibullying programs. It is important for parents to model positive social behavior for their children, offer advice about how to

Having open communication with a parent or guardian can make discussing bullying easier for a teen.

respond to bullying, and encourage their children to seek help, if needed. They should also teach their children to be assertive and encourage them to defend their peers who are being bullied.

But before parents can help their bullied children, they must be aware of the situation. This may be difficult if the children are too afraid or embarrassed to talk about the bullying. Educator Joan Lowell urges parents to ask questions about a child's day and be alert to signs that suggest bullying. According to counselor

Raychelle Lohmann, signs can include things such as withdrawing from or losing interest in school activities and events, missing school, having more headaches or stomachaches than usual, significant changes in mood or sleep patterns, or unexplained injuries such as scrapes or bruises. When communicating with a child, parents should stress that it is important to tell an adult about bullying in order to get help and that this is not tattling but rather staying safe. They can ask whether other kids may have seen the bullying incidents and get those kids' input as well.

Lohmann counsels that, rather than trying to fix things, parents should listen to their children and provide support and validation. A child should feel comfortable talking to his or her parents about the situation. But the parents should also make the school aware of what's going on. This involves advance preparation, such as collecting and documenting information about the incidents. They should try to determine how long the bullying has been occurring, who the bullies are, exactly what is happening, and when and

> "PARENTAL CARE AND SUPPORT ARE THE MOST EFFECTIVE WAYS BY WHICH VICTIMS COPE WITH BULLYING."[3]
>
> —LEANNE LESTER AND COLLEAGUES, AUTHORS OF A 2017 STUDY ON SCHOOL BULLYING INTERVENTION

where it is happening. If the problem is cyberbullying, documentation includes texts, emails, and screenshots. Parents should make an appointment with the principal and take the documentation, but the child or teen who has been bullied should describe the situation and explain what he or she needs to feel safe. Fixing the situation does not include parents meeting with the bully; this is the school's job.

The parents' goal should be to make sure their child feels safe. Parents can teach their kids techniques for gaining self-confidence. For example, they can emphasize their child's strengths and talents. If appropriate, parents should seek professional counseling for the child to address psychological issues arising from the bullying. And they should always follow up with the school and with their child to ensure that the problem has been addressed.

> "WE NEED TO ALWAYS REMEMBER THE POWER OF ACCEPTANCE AND KINDNESS. BEYOND THE SCOPE OF BULLYING, WE NEED TO INSTILL IN OUR KIDS THAT WORDS AND ACTIONS DO MATTER, AND MOST IMPORTANTLY, THAT WE REALLY CAN MAKE A POSITIVE DIFFERENCE IN SOMEONE'S LIFE."[4]
>
> —RAYCHELLE LOHMANN, AUTHOR AND TEEN COUNSELOR

WHAT TEENS CAN DO

Bullied teens often feel helpless, but they are not. While victims or targets may not be able to stop the bullying, they can control their reactions to it. It helps to try to understand the motivations for the bully's actions. Looking at the situation from the outside can provide a new perspective—it enables targets to realize that bullies have their own reasons for behaving badly and that the targets are not responsible for the situation.

A bullied person may feel many negative emotions, such as fear, anger, anxiety, sadness, and depression. These feelings are valid. However, it is important not to make decisions when feeling this way. Talking to a parent or other trusted adult, or getting counseling, can help the bullied kid work through these emotions and make positive choices.

TIPS FOR OVERCOMING BULLYING

Standing up to a bully is hard, but having a plan and knowing what to do helps. Experts have tips that can help teens deal with and overcome bullying. First, people can try to understand the bully's mindset. Why is he or she acting like this? A person can also speak to the bully if he or she feels safe doing so. People can seek advice from someone, preferably an adult, to help them deal with the situation and stress that it causes. People who experience bullying shouldn't blame themselves for the bully's behavior. They should focus on ways to keep their physical and mental health in good condition and should seek out role models who have overcome bullying.

Spending time with friends is a good reminder for bullying victims that they are not alone.

Social support from parents, teachers, and classmates can help protect youth who are bullied from experiencing negative outcomes.

The bullied person should learn to manage stress. This is a time to rely on friends and family rather than isolating oneself. Getting out, doing fun activities, and taking up a new hobby or interest can take the person's mind off the bullying problem and make him or her happier. Engaging in a calming activity such as yoga or meditation can decrease stress.

As the target becomes more self-confident and overcomes the negative effects of bullying, he or she may want to use the skills and information gained to help others who are experiencing the same thing. For example, the person might volunteer at an antibullying organization, set up a school support group, or write about his or her experiences.

People will always have problems and stresses in their lives, and some will react to these problems by lashing out and bullying others. Antibullying programs and the development of school environments that are safe, positive, and inclusive can go a long way toward controlling bullying. But it may persist, to some extent, throughout people's lives. Adults bully and get bullied, too, and the antibullying skills kids learn in school may be equally useful in their adult lives.

ADULT BULLYING

Adults can be bullies too. If an individual sees an adult who exhibits bullying behavior only once in a while, it is best to only interact when necessary and then immediately leave. Dealing with a chronic bully—one with whom a person has constant, daily contact—is harder. People should document every interaction with the bully. This information should include dates, times, locations, and circumstances where the bullying takes place. The person should write down exact quotes and ask witnesses to do the same. This information can be used in formal complaints or legal action, if necessary. A chronic bully often targets multiple people. If the targets band together this may cause the bully to back off.

If teachers are educated about bullying, they can take steps to observe student behavior and stop bullying in the future.

CHAPTER NINE

PROMISING RESEARCH

As the definition and description of bullying has grown more precise, research has expanded to consider the impacts of bullying on specific groups. These include teens in alternative high schools, Native American teens, LGBTQ adolescents, and Black adolescents. A 2016 study by the National Academies of Sciences, Engineering, and Medicine stresses that because of the consequences of bullying on physical and psychological health, bullying prevention research should be a public health priority.

However, much more research on the bullying of specific groups is necessary. Dr. Frederick Rivara is part of the committee that authored the 2016 study. He states that further research is needed regarding bullying of high-risk groups, such as LGBTQ individuals, youth with disabilities, and obese youth. He points out that, because of the differences in people being bullied, there will likely need to be specific interventions for different groups. Overall, the report says that more evidence-based research is needed to develop antibullying policies. Current research shows that some existing policies, such as zero-tolerance measures resulting in suspension or expulsion, do not always decrease bullying. More data is also needed on the effectiveness of state laws in controlling bullying. Rivara states that many school and community intervention programs are effective, particularly those that involve not just students and teachers, but also parents, bus drivers, and others. Working together, these members of the school community can create a positive climate that discourages bullying.

As research continues, methods for controlling and preventing bullying are trending in two directions. One direction involves methods grounded in psychology and sociology. The other involves technology.

SKILLS THAT BULLIES NEED TO HEAL

Changing bullies' habits is possible, but they must be taught the skills to behave in more positive ways. They need to understand that bullying is a choice and learn to take responsibility for their actions. They must learn empathy in order to understand how bullying makes victims feel. Many bullies need to learn techniques for better anger management and impulse control. Finally, bullies must be taught that all people deserve respect. Parents, school counselors, teachers, or peers can show bullies how to help and support weaker kids rather than bully them.

EMPOWERING BYSTANDERS

Bullying is considered an adverse childhood experience (ACE). This is an experience that can lead to future violence and victimization, and likely to lifelong physical and psychological health problems. In someone who is bullied, the amygdala, the region of the brain housing the fight-or-flight response, becomes overactive. The person becomes hypervigilant, and the amygdala stays active most or all of the time. This triggers anxiety and depression and stifles higher brain functions, such as planning, decision-making, and conflict resolution. Bullied people see themselves as victims and go into survival mode—they react from instinct and emotion and find it difficult to think clearly or process information. It is a difficult mindset to change.

WHAT EDUCATORS CAN DO

Educators want to be a force for good in their classrooms and schools, but it is often difficult to know how to deal with bullying. Several general approaches can help. For instance, teachers can teach kindness and empathy. They can also help students connect with their peers and teach them ways to stand up for themselves. In addition, it's helpful for teachers to notice and stop behaviors that may lead to bullying. These behaviors include rolling one's eyes, staring, laughing cruelly, calling people names, and excluding people. Teachers can also use the arts, such as literature, drama, and visual arts, to present different perspectives and encourage people to be more tolerant of others.

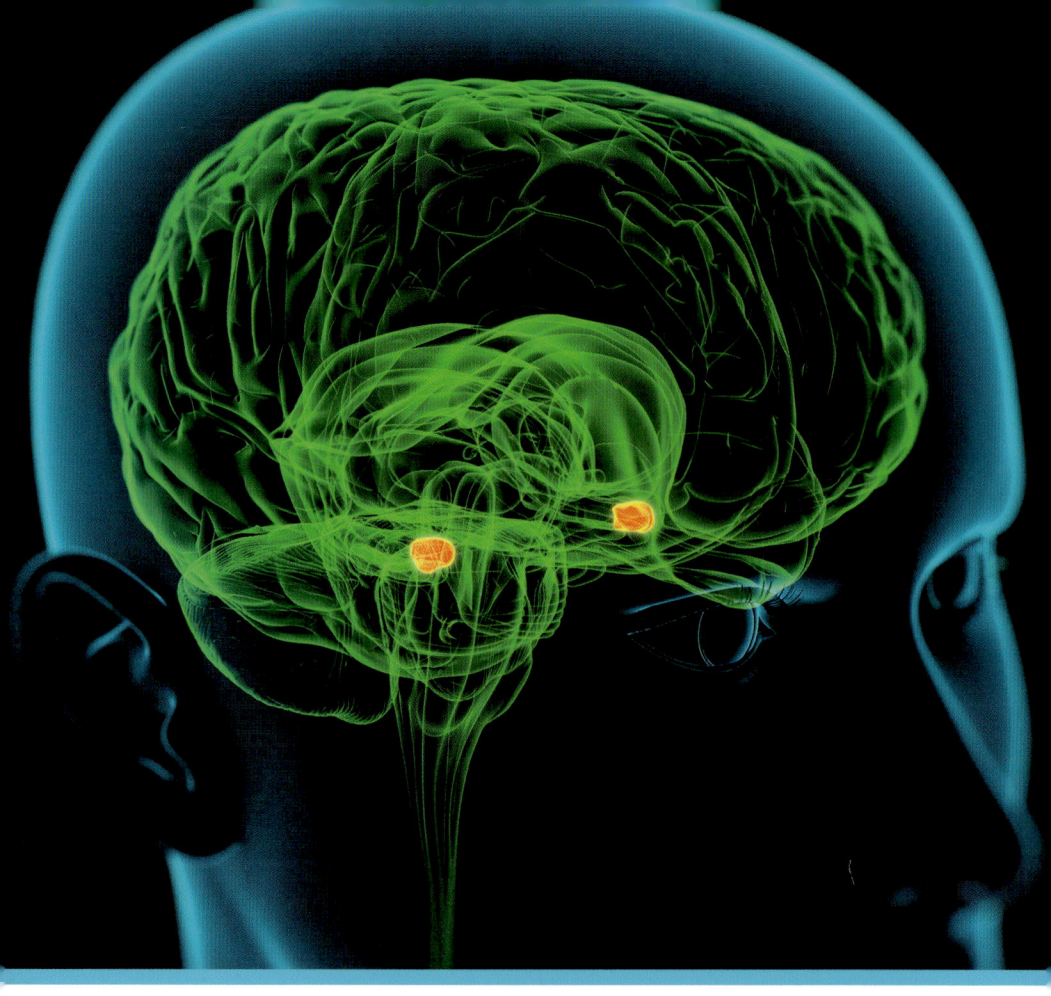

The amygdalae, shown in orange, respond to stress. These parts of the brain can become extremely sensitive in bullying victims.

Students can make a difference at their school and anywhere else they might encounter bullying. Studies have shown the effectiveness of bystanders standing up for bullied victims, which can help stop the bullying incident. Thus, educators and social work professionals are beginning to feel that the best way to resolve bullying incidents is to educate and empower bystanders. In addition to setting antibullying policies, many schools are now beginning to train bystanders to respond actively and take responsibility for trying to stop the bullying. Simply objecting to the bully's actions and urging their friends to do the same can change the power dynamic and make the victim feel less helpless. When bystanders show inclusivity, responsibility, and empathy toward the bullied child or teen, they send a positive message to everyone involved in the incident. They help bullied targets understand that the problem lies with the bully, not with them.

TECHNOLOGY AND BULLYING

Improved technology has led to the rapidly growing trend of cyberbullying. Scientists think technology will also be the key to controlling this form of bullying. There are too many posts for social network employees to manually review them for cruel content. So, artificial intelligence (AI) is being used to detect words and phrases that suggest bullying. Since 2017, Instagram has been using a bullying filter that detects and hides mean

> "I ALLOWED MYSELF TO BE BULLIED BECAUSE I WAS SCARED AND DIDN'T KNOW HOW TO DEFEND MYSELF. I WAS BULLIED UNTIL I PREVENTED A NEW STUDENT FROM BEING BULLIED. BY STANDING UP FOR HIM, I LEARNED TO STAND UP FOR MYSELF."[1]
>
> —JACKIE CHAN, MARTIAL ARTIST AND ACTOR

While technology might help decrease cyberbullying, it's important for teens to tell a trusted adult about the bullying whenever it occurs.

comments. It has also added AI that detects attacks on people's character or appearance and looks for threats that occur in photographs or captions. The company says this active approach is necessary, since many users do not report the cyberbullying. This way, the company can take action against repeat offenders. However, cyberbullies can still reach their victims by creating new, anonymous profiles from which to send hateful messages.

AI also has the potential to be very useful in off-line bullying. Bullying and discrimination against women are rampant in technology firms in the United States and Europe. An intelligent program named Spot is being used to help victims of this workplace abuse report harassment safely and securely. It provides a time-stamped record of the incident, usually in the form of a victim interview, which can later be used as evidence against the bully.

Another tool, called Botler AI, provides advice to people who have

USING AI TO TARGET CYBERBULLIES

Gilles Jacobs is a language researcher at Ghent University in Belgium. His team is using a machine learning algorithm to spot words and phrases related to bullying. On one social networking site, the algorithm detected and blocked almost two-thirds of insulting words and phrases in 114,000 posts.[2] But the tool has trouble detecting sarcastic remarks, and it cannot simply remove all remarks using offensive language, because not all of these are bullying. Another study at McGill University in Montreal, Canada, uses an algorithm to recognize speech aimed at certain groups targeted by bullies, including women, Black people, and people who are overweight. Research leader Haji Saleem says these specific hate speech filters are more accurate than general keyword filters. The algorithm also detected more subtle abuse, such as using the word "animals" to dehumanize targets.

been sexually harassed. It has been trained by compiling hundreds of thousands of court case documents on sexual harassment from the United States and Canada. By comparing the language of a submitted harassment case with the language of these documents, it can analyze whether a victim has been sexually harassed in the eyes of the law. It produces a written incident report that can be given to human resources departments or to the police. The first version of Botler AI was active for six months and achieved 89 percent accuracy. Botler AI's founder, Amir Moravej, says, "One of our users was sexually assaulted by a politician and said the tool gave her the confidence she needed and empowered her to take action."[3] The user began legal proceedings against the politician. Teaching this bot the language of bullying, instead of sexual harassment, could result in an impressive tool for tackling the menace of cyberbullying.

Bullying is as old as civilization. It seems to

> "AN IMPORTANT POINT TO MAKE HERE IS WHILE BULLYING HAS EXISTED FOR EONS, SOCIETY HAS PROGRESSED TO REALIZE THAT WE CAN NO LONGER ACCEPT IT AS A NORMAL PART OF GROWING UP BECAUSE IT'S NOT."[4]
>
> —DR. FREDERICK RIVARA, CHAIR OF A COMMITTEE COMPILING THE 2016 REPORT ON BULLYING BY THE NATIONAL ACADEMIES OF SCIENCES, ENGINEERING, AND MEDICINE

Antibullying movements are gaining attention around the world.

be a part of human nature, and that means it will always exist. But like other negative human behaviors, bullying can be controlled and its negative impacts minimized. As author Megan Kelley Hall said, "School administrators can't say it's up to the parents. Parents can't say it's up to the teachers. Teachers can't say it's not their job. And kids can't say, 'I was too afraid to tell.' Every single one of us has to play our role if we're serious about putting an end to the madness. We are all responsible. We must be."[5] In short, it is up to every person involved to be a part of the solution to bullying.

ESSENTIAL FACTS

FACTS ABOUT BULLYING

- Bullying is cruel or hurtful treatment of another person. Three characteristics set it apart from actions such as teasing. First, there is an imbalance of power. Second, the cruel behavior is repeated over and over. Third, the actions are not accidental; the bully deliberately chooses to harm the target.
- Bullying can be physical, verbal, or emotional. It can occur in person or online.
- Bullies may target people who are different from them. People are sometimes targeted on the basis of sexual orientation, race or ethnicity, religion, or physical characteristics.

IMPACT ON DAILY LIFE

- Bullying can make the target's daily life miserable. The target can be filled with fear, shame, and humiliation. He or she may hide or otherwise try to avoid the bully.
- Bullied people of any age may suffer from physical and psychological problems.

- Bullies may have lifelong problems with relationships, difficulty holding a job, and psychological problems. They are more likely to commit crimes than people who aren't bullies.

DEALING WITH BULLYING

- Teaching kids about empathy and kindness from an early age can prevent bullying. When children can see a situation from another's point of view, they are less likely to treat others badly.
- Teens can manage their stress, talk to a trusted adult, or even stand up to the bully in the moment. They can work with adults and friends to plan ways to deal with the situation.

QUOTE

"Bullying is an attempt to instill fear and self-loathing. Being the repetitive target of bullying damages your ability to view yourself as a desirable, capable and effective individual."

—Dr. Mark Dombeck, *American Academy of Experts in Traumatic Stress*

GLOSSARY

bystander
A person who is present at an event or incident but doesn't participate or intervene.

capitalistic
Having to do with an economic system in which businesses are privately owned and operated for the purpose of making a profit.

contemporary
Occurring during the same time.

learned helplessness
A psychological condition in which a person feels powerless to change the situation and gives up, feeling there is no way out.

ostracize
To be shunned or otherwise excluded from a society or a group.

prejudice
An unfair feeling of dislike for a person or group because of race, sex, or religion.

racism
Inferior treatment of a person or group of people based on race.

risk factor
Something that raises a person's susceptibility to something harmful.

stereotype
A widely held but oversimplified idea about a particular type of person or thing.

truancy
Staying away from school without a good excuse.

ADDITIONAL RESOURCES

SELECTED BIBLIOGRAPHY

Koo, Hyojin. "A Time Line of the Evolution of School Bullying in Differing Social Contexts." *Education Research Institute*, 2007, files.eric.ed.gov. Accessed 9 June 2020.

McGill, Natalie. "More Research Needed to Prevent, Understand Bullying, Report Finds." *APHA*, Aug. 2016, thenationshealth.aphapublications.org. Accessed 9 June 2020.

"What Is Bullying?" *Stop Bullying*, 30 May 2019, stopbullying.gov. Accessed 9 June 2020.

FURTHER READINGS

Berg, Shannon. *Surviving and Thriving at School*. Abdo, 2021.

Miller, Marie-Therese, PhD. *Handling Depression*. Abdo, 2022.

Rusick, Jessica. *#IAmAWitness: Confronting Bullying*. Abdo, 2020.

ONLINE RESOURCES

Booklinks
NONFICTION NETWORK
FREE ONLINE NONFICTION RESOURCES

To learn more about bullying, please visit **abdobooklinks.com** or scan this QR code. These links are routinely monitored and updated to provide the most current information available.

MORE INFORMATION

For more information on this subject, contact or visit the following organizations:

PACER's National Bullying Prevention Center

8161 Normandale Blvd.
Minneapolis, MN 55437
952-838-9000
pacer.org/bullying

PACER provides clear, concise information on bullying prevention, including online questions and answers, facts and statistics on bullying, and videos, stories, and classroom resources.

Stop Bullying

200 Independence Ave. SW
Washington, DC 20201
stopbullying.gov

Stop Bullying is run by the US Department of Health and Human Services. It collects and provides information from different government agencies about what bullying and cyberbullying are, who is at risk, and how to prevent and respond to bullying. The site has educational resources and a blog.

SOURCE NOTES

CHAPTER 1. BEING BULLIED

1. Marcela Rojas. "From Bullied to Bravery: One Girl's Story." *USA Today*, 24 Oct. 2013, usatoday.com. Accessed 24 Aug. 2020.
2. Sherri Gordon. "An Overview of Bullying." *Verywell Family*, 24 Oct. 2019, verywellfamily.com. Accessed 24 Aug. 2020.
3. Catherine P. Bradshaw et al. "Bullying and Peer Victimization at School: Perceptual Differences Between Students and School Staff." *Johns Hopkins University*, 2007, jhu.pure.elsevier.com. Accessed 24 Aug. 2020.
4. Mary C. Lamia. "Do Bullies Really Have Low Self-Esteem?" *Psychology Today*, 22 Oct. 2010, psychologytoday.com. Accessed 24 Aug. 2020.
5. Elizabeth Thomas. "Cyberbullying Is on the Rise Among Middle and High School Students, Report Finds." *ABC News*, 16 July 2019, abcnews.go.com. Accessed 24 Aug. 2020.
6. Sally Ho. "Girls Report More Harassment Amid Rise in US Cyberbullying." *Dispatch*, 26 July 2019, cdispatch.com. Accessed 24 Aug. 2020.

CHAPTER 2. WHAT IS BULLYING?

1. Sherri Gordon. "How to Deal with Teasing and Subtle Forms of Bullying." *Verywell Family*, 30 Sept. 2019, verywellfamily.com. Accessed 24 Aug. 2020.
2. "What Is Hazing?" *University of Michigan*, n.d., deanofstudents.umich.edu. Accessed 24 Aug. 2020.
3. "What Is Bullying?" *Stop Bullying*, 21 July 2020, stopbullying.gov. Accessed 24 Aug. 2020.
4. Kelly Oakes. "Why Children Become Bullies at School." *BBC*, 15 Sept. 2019, bbc.com. Accessed 24 Aug. 2020.
5. Luna C. M. Centifanti. "Types of Relational Aggression in Girls Are Differentiated by Callous-Unemotional Traits, Peers and Parental Overcontrol." *NCBI*, 13 Nov. 2015, ncbi.nlm.nih.gov. Accessed 24 Aug. 2020.
6. "What Is Cyberbullying?" *Stop Bullying*, 21 July 2020, stopbullying.gov. Accessed 24 Aug. 2020.

7. Brianna Flavin. "Is Cyberbullying Illegal? When Comments Turn Criminal." *Rasmussen College*, 25 Apr. 2017, rasmussen.edu. Accessed 24 Aug. 2020.
8. Ryan Blitstein. "Bullying: A Junior Hate Crime?" *Pacific Standard*, 14 June 2017, psmag.com. Accessed 24 Aug. 2020.

CHAPTER 3. EFFECTS OF BULLYING

1. "The Issue of Bullying." *Stomp Out Bullying*, n.d., stompoutbullying.org. Accessed 24 Aug. 2020.
2. "The Relationship between Bullying and Suicide." *CDC*, n.d., cdc.gov. Accessed 24 Aug. 2020.
3. Mark Dombeck. "The Long Term Effects of Bullying." *American Academy of Experts in Traumatic Stress*, 2020, aaets.org. Accessed 24 Aug. 2020.
4. Dieter Wolke and Suzet Tanya Lereya. "Long-Term Effects of Bullying." *NCBI*, Sept. 2015, ncbi.nlm.nih.gov. Accessed 24 Aug. 2020.
5. "Bullying: How Parents Can Help." *Mayo Clinic*, 28 Aug. 2019, mayoclinic.org. Accessed 24 Aug. 2020.
6. Ryan Walker. "I'm a Teenager Who Was Bullied: Here's What Bullying among Teens Looks Like Today." *Parents*, 20 Nov. 2019, parents.com. Accessed 24 Aug. 2020.

CHAPTER 4. WHO GETS BULLIED?

1. Bertrand Russell. *Education and the Social Order.* Allen and Unwin, 1977. 23.
2. Sherri Gordon. "3 Types of Prejudicial Bullying." *Verywell Family*, 20 June 2020, verywellfamily.com. Accessed 24 Aug. 2020.
3. "LGBTQ Youth." *Stop Bullying*, 21 Sept. 2017, stopbullying.gov. Accessed 24 Aug. 2020.
4. Ashley Strickland. "Bullying Is a 'Serious Public Health Problem,' Experts Say." *CNN*, 21 June 2017, cnn.com. Accessed 24 Aug. 2020.

CHAPTER 5. WHY DOES BULLYING HAPPEN?

1. Katherine Lee. "Why It's Important to Nurture Empathy in Kids." *Verywell Family*, 14 June 2020, verywellfamily.com. Accessed 24 Aug. 2020.

SOURCE NOTES CONTINUED

2. "Why Kids Become Bullies." *Yale Medicine*, 28 Feb. 2017, yalemedicine.org. Accessed 24 Aug. 2020.
3. Sherri Gordon. "5 Subtly Mean Phrases Bullies Use." *Verywell Family*, 5 June 2019, verywellfamily.com. Accessed 24 Aug. 2020.
4. "What Kids Can Do." *Stop Bullying*, 28 Sept. 2017, stopbullying.gov. Accessed 24 Aug. 2020.
5. "What Kids Can Do."
6. Hogan Sherrow. "The Origins of Bullying." *Scientific American*, 15 Dec. 2011, scientificamerican.com. Accessed 24 Aug. 2020.

CHAPTER 6. A HISTORY OF BULLYING

1. Hyojin Koo. "A Time Line of the Evolution of School Bullying in Different Social Contexts." *Asia Pacific Education Review*, 2017, files.eric.ed.gov. Accessed 24 Aug. 2020.
2. Koo, "A Time Line of the Evolution of School Bullying."
3. Koo, "A Time Line of the Evolution of School Bullying."
4. Douglas Harper. "Bully." *Online Etymology Dictionary*, n.d., etymonline.com. Accessed 24 Aug. 2020.
5. Koo, "A Time Line of the Evolution of School Bullying."
6. Koo, "A Time Line of the Evolution of School Bullying."
7. Koo, "A Time Line of the Evolution of School Bullying."
8. Hogan Sherrow. "The Origins of Bullying." *Scientific American*, 15 Dec. 2011, scientificamerican.com. Accessed 24 Aug. 2020.

CHAPTER 7. THE BULLY AND THE BYSTANDER

1. "Bystanders to Bullying." *Stop Bullying*, 23 Oct. 2018, stopbullying.gov. Accessed 24 Aug. 2020.
2. "Facts about Bullying." *Stop Bullying*, 12 Aug. 2020, stopbullying.gov. Accessed 24 Aug. 2020.
3. "Peers and Bullying: Tattling vs. Telling." *Safe@School*, n.d., safeatschool.ca. Accessed 24 Aug. 2020.
4. "Bullying." *Psychology Today*, n.d., psychologytoday.com. Accessed 24 Aug. 2020.
5. "Bullying Statistics." *PACER*, n.d., pacer.org. Accessed 24 Aug. 2020.

6. William E. Copeland et al. "Adult Psychiatric Outcomes of Bullying and Being Bullied by Peers in Childhood and Adolescence." *JAMA Psychiatry*, 2013, jamanetwork.com. Accessed 24 Aug. 2020.
7. Lorna Blumen. "How Does Bullying Affect the Bully?" *Bullying Epidemic*, 16 May 2013, bullyingepidemic.com. Accessed 24 Aug. 2020.
8. Rebecca Fraser-Thill. "How Being a Bully Affects Future Development." *Verywell Family*, 1 June 2020, verywellfamily.com. Accessed 24 Aug. 2020.
9. Blumen, "How Does Bullying Affect the Bully?"
10. "Bullies, Victims, and Bystanders: Types of Bully Bystanders." *Health*, 31 Jan. 2014, athealth.com. Accessed 24 Aug. 2020.

CHAPTER 8. OVERCOMING BULLYING

1. Dan Olweus. "The Olweus Bully/Victim Questionnaire." *Research Gate*, Jan. 1996, researchgate.net. Accessed 24 Aug. 2020.
2. Dan Olweus and Susan P. Limber. "Bullying in School." *Wiley Online Library*, 9 Apr. 2010, onlinelibrary.wiley.com. Accessed 24 Aug. 2020.
3. Leanne Lester et al. "Family Involvement in a Whole-School Bullying Intervention." *Springer Link*, 5 June 2017, link.springer.com. Accessed 24 Aug. 2020.
4. Raychelle Cassada Lohmann. "What to Do When Your Teen Is Being Bullied in School." *US News & World Report*, 30 Oct. 2018, health.usnews.com. Accessed 24 Aug. 2020.

CHAPTER 9. PROMISING RESEARCH

1. Mason Komay. "Anti-Bullying and Bullying Quotes to Remember." *Better Help*, 7 Nov. 2019, betterhelp.com. Accessed 24 Aug. 2020.
2. Sarah Griffiths. "Can This Technology Put an End to Bullying?" *BBC*, 10 Feb. 2019, bbc.com. Accessed 24 Aug. 2020.
3. Griffiths, "Can This Technology Put an End to Bullying?"
4. Natalie McGill. "More Research Needed to Prevent, Understand Bullying, Report Finds." *Nation's Health*, Aug. 2016, thenationshealth.aphapublications.org. Accessed 24 Aug. 2020.
5. Komay, "Anti-Bullying and Bullying Quotes to Remember."

INDEX

adults, 22, 28, 87
anxiety, 25–27, 30–33, 39, 65, 69, 71, 73, 87, 93
artificial intelligence (AI), 95–98
assault, 14, 16, 28, 39, 61, 98

bullying culture, 68, 74
bully-victims, 31–32, 51, 69, 71, 83
Bureau of Justice Statistics, 14
bystanders, 10, 13, 15, 17, 22, 25, 45, 51, 54, 67–68, 72–73, 77, 94–95

Carter, Ruth, 20
Centers for Disease Control and Prevention (CDC), 28
Choson Dynasty, 61
counselor, 7, 29, 84, 86, 92
cyberbullying, 11, 15, 17–19, 26, 29, 36, 54, 59, 65, 67, 85, 95–96, 98

depression, 26–27, 29–31, 39, 44, 69, 71, 73, 87, 93
discrimination, 19, 39, 77, 97
diversity, 39, 42, 51, 75
Donegan, Richard, 58–59

empathy, 17, 48, 50–51, 54, 71, 75, 92–93, 95
Englander, Elizabeth, 21, 40
Equality and Human Rights Commission, 42

Gordon, Sherri, 9, 13, 21, 40
grades, 25–26

harassment, 15, 18, 20–21, 40, 42, 51, 61–62, 97–98
hate crimes, 39–40
hazing, 13–14, 61
headaches, 27, 85
homophobia, 77

ijime, 61
isolation, 32, 35, 39, 61–62, 71, 77, 88

JAMA Psychiatry, 69, 71
jealousy, 21, 36, 47–48, 51

Koo, Hyojin, 59, 62, 64

Lamia, Mary C., 10
learned helplessness, 27
Lereya, Suzet Tanya, 30
LGBTQ, 20, 22, 26, 29, 35, 40–41, 91

middle school, 11, 68, 71, 81
minorities, 6, 39

National Academies of Sciences, Engineering, and Medicine, 43, 91, 98
National Center for Education Statistics, 11, 14

Olweus, Dan, 63, 79, 83
Olweus Bullying Prevention Program (OBPP), 79–83
ostracizing, 15, 61–62, 68

Parsons, Rehtaeh, 28
peer pressure, 50
physical bullying, 14–16, 37, 61, 63, 68
physical disability, 6, 37
popularity, 5, 35–36, 47–48, 57
post-traumatic stress disorder (PTSD), 31
power, 9, 13–14, 21, 27, 33, 37, 47–48, 50, 54, 59, 62–64, 72, 95
prejudice, 22, 37, 40, 43
prejudicial bullying, 15, 20, 22, 37, 39–40, 42–43, 49–50
Prince, Phoebe, 28

questionnaire, 81–82

race, 15, 19, 22, 35, 37, 39–40
relational aggression, 14, 16–17, 37, 51, 68
religion, 6, 15, 19, 22, 35, 39–40, 42, 77
risk factors, 28–29, 47, 49
Rivara, Frederick, 43, 91–92, 98
rumors, 9, 15, 21, 36, 68

school community, 25, 92
School Psychology Review, 10
self-confidence, 7, 21, 25, 33, 86, 88
self-esteem, 10, 26, 39
sexism, 77
sexting, 20
sexual bullying, 15, 20–22
sexual orientation, 6, 15, 20, 40, 42
sleeping disorder, 26
social media, 7, 15, 18–19, 21, 51, 58
Steele, Ann, 73
stereotypes, 22
stomachaches, 27, 85
Stop Bullying, 19, 40, 53–54, 67
stress, 28–29, 44, 65, 87–89
substance abuse, 26, 31, 44
suicide, 28–31, 44, 62, 65
symptoms, 25–27

teasing, 9, 13, 17, 35, 48, 81
Tom Brown's Schooldays, 57, 61

ulcers, 27
United Nations, 62
University of Michigan, 14

verbal bullying, 14–17, 37, 52

withdrawn, 26
Wolke, Dieter, 30
workplace bullying, 63
World Journal of Psychiatry, 26
World War II, 62–63

ABOUT THE AUTHOR

CAROL HAND

Carol Hand has a PhD in zoology. She has taught college biology and written biology assessments, middle and high school science curricula, and more than 70 young adult science books, including several on topics related to health and the social sciences. Currently she works as a freelance writer.

ABOUT THE CONSULTANT

DR. SAMANTHA COYLE

Dr. Samantha Coyle is an assistant professor in the psychology department at Montclair State University. Her research investigates the impact of bullying-victimization on social-emotional and academic performance of youth and protective factors, such as social support, for victims of bullying. Dr. Coyle's work has been published in highly regarded journals in the field including *Psychological Bulletin*, *Journal of School Psychology*, and *School Psychology Review*.